THE UPFOLD WITCH

Who first cast Celia Wainwright in the rôle of the Upfold Witch, and why and how did she disappear one night in 1953? What connection was there between her and young Julian Farnham? Why, on the day after she disappeared, did her husband, elderly Mr Wainwright, suddenly leave their home at Mulberry Cottage never to return? What, in fact, is the mystery which hangs over Mulberry Cottage and which has led it to lie vacant for nearly ten years?

Fascinated by the sinister rumours which circulated among the villagers, the new owners of the cottage uncovered a distasteful piece of village history, which included persecution, murder and bigamy.

BY JOSEPHINE BELL

Detective Novels

Novels

Non-Fiction

THE UPFOLD WITCH

by

JOSEPHINE BELL

HODDER AND STOUGHTON

Copyright © 1964 by D. B. Ball

First printed 1964

Printed in Great Britain for Hodder and Stoughton Limited, St. Paul's House, Warwick Lane, London E.C.4, by Northumberland Press Ltd., Gateshead

PROLOGUE

On an autumn night in the year 1953 two men walked down a mist-covered lane on the outskirts of the village of Upfold in the Sussex Weald.

They were both young men, country folk, broad-shouldered and stocky. Their rubber, knee-high boots, damp and mud-clogged, made no sound on the road. They carried guns, because one of them, George Cutfield, was a farmer whose sheep had been attacked recently by a rogue dog, so far unidentified. He and a friend Pawley, the local butcher, were making a night of it, patrolling the fields and lanes, in the hope of flushing the marauder if it were lurking around. But they had seen no wandering dog; the land had been peaceful under a full moon on the higher ground. It was only in the hollows and the hedgerows and the sunk lanes that the mist swirled patchily.

They came to the outskirts of the village and to the first of the houses, isolated cottages for the most part, several of them owned by weekend people from the towns, even from London. Two had been enlarged, one with a built-on studio, the other by joining together a former small pair of dwellings. One had been disfigured by the addition of a heavy thatch that gave it the appearance of wearing an enormous, grotesque straw hat, an incongruity that caused some aesthetic indignation, a good deal of laughter in the village and a peculiar pride on the part of the owners. Not far away from this monstrosity stood a very charming small house in a beautiful garden. It was called Mulberry Cottage and there really was a mulberry tree on the lawn.

Cutfield and Pawley were nearing the gate of this house

5

when they heard a car coming along the lane, though the mist was too thick to see it. The unseen driver changed gear, clumsily.

"It's her," Cutfield said, quickly.

"Look out she don't run us down," Pawley answered.

The small garden gate leading to the front door of the house was beside them. The wider opening to the garage was beyond. The car would have to pass. Without another word Cutfield opened the small gate and went through. His friend followed.

Inside the hedge the mist was thinner. The two men could see a vague outline of the front of the house and the door. They could also see the dark mass of the garage. Above ground level the house was clear in the moon-light.

The car, continuing to slow down, passed the small gate, turned, grinding another gear, into the short straight drive to the garage and stopped, apparently just short of it.

"Been out on the tiles," Cutfield muttered to his friend. "Up at Farnham's, I reckon."

"Boozing as well," Pawley whispered back. "She don't usually drive that bad."

They crouched down by the hedge as a figure moved from the side of the car. In the enveloping mist it was a strange sight, bulky, irregular, swaying as it moved slowly towards the house.

"My God!" Cutfield breathed. "What in heaven's name has she got with her?"

"Devil's work," Pawley answered. "More of her devil's work."

The apparition reached the door and now, despite the mist, the watchers understood. For one figure, small and slight and wrapped in a rug or blanket, was laid on the single step and another figure, tall and angular, fumbled a key in the lock and having opened the door, picked up his former burden and went inside. Another pause and the door was

6

shut. A short interval and a light went on in an upstairs room.

"Well, I'm dammed," Pawley said. "Young Mr Farnham's brought her home blotto, and now he's putting her to bed."

He slapped his thigh, suppressing a belly laugh with difficulty. But Cutfield clutched his arm and pointed. The bedroom light had gone out.

"Stopping on, is he?" Pawley's laugh rocked him again. "Without any co-operation, the dirty young dog!"

"No," Cutfield said, urgently, suppressing his own bawdy conclusions. "No, he isn't. He's leaving. And he's got the rug with him."

It was true. The door opened silently and Farnham looked out, peering through the light mist that still wreathed the door but was stirring now as the breeze began to blow down the lane.

The two men, crouching again and silent, watched the tall figure of the young man move towards the garage. They heard him start the car and drive it in. The mist was clearing fast. Farnham appeared again, pulled the garage doors together and secured them with the padlock that hung from one of them. Then, with a shrinking, strange look on his face, turned towards the silent house, he went out of the garage drive, leaving those gates open as he had found them and turned towards his home, passing within only a few feet of the astonished onlookers, crouched still behind the hedge inside the garden gate. They saw that he had the rug hanging from his arm. Obviously it was his own.

When the sound of his footsteps had died away the two men rose to their feet, staring at one another.

"Did you see the look on his face?" Cutfield asked. Though they were now alone he still spoke in a voice hardly above a whisper.

"I did, that," Pawley answered. He got out a handkerchief to wipe his own forehead.

"I don't like the look of it," Cutfield went on. "Mr Wain-

7

right's away till the end of the week, he told me. Young Mr Farnham can't have done more than pop her into bed. If she's ill or anything . . ."

"He'd have sent for the doctor at his own place," Pawley answered. "She can look after herself, can't she?"

He was itching to be gone. He never felt comfortable near Mulberry Cottage. He now felt very uncomfortable indeed.

Cutfield moved forward towards the house.

"You're never going to bring *her* down?" Pawley almost shouted. He was prepared to run for it if his friend persisted in such madness.

Cutfield turned. His face was grim, clear-cut in the moonlight that shone on the whole front of the house now that the mist had blown away.

"Don't be a fool," he said. "You saw Farnham's face, didn't you? There's something wrong here. I owe it to Mr Wainwright to check up it's not serious. He did a lot for me in the spring when Dad died and I had all that on my hands."

Pawley knew what his friend meant. The farm had gone down badly in old Cutfield's last years. An obstinate old codger, against any improvements. Mr Wainwright had put up money, not only advice. Bought the farm and handed it back to George to manage and buy in again on easy terms. Generous.

"All the same," he protested feebly, "She won't thank you. Don't see her coming down, the way she was when he carted her in."

Cutfield did not answer. He had no intention of ringing the bell or knocking. He tried the front door, found it locked and walked round to the back. That door was locked too, but looking up he saw the bathroom window open above the sloping roof of the coal shed. By the time Pawley had followed him round he was up on this roof, pushing the window further open.

8

"Come on!" he called down, softly. "I can't do this on my own."

Pawley grunted. There were many reasons why his friend should not go into this dreaded house alone, his reputation, his position with his wife, not altogether easy at any time, above all the possible danger from *her* to him, personally. Even in Pawley's own mind, as in the minds of so many others in Upfold, Mrs Wainright's name was never used, except perhaps to strangers.

So, very reluctantly, he levered himself on to the sloping roof of the shed, using the water-butt that Cutfield had stepped from. The two men scrambled quietly into the bathroom, tiptoed out on to the landing and reached the door of the room that looked out at the front of the house. They moved remarkably silently, but they were country-bred and had spent much time on other nights in their not-distant youth poaching various game in the neighbouring fields and woods.

Cutfield opened the door without a sound. Pawley looked over his shoulder.

Celia Wainwright lay on her back in the bed, covered up to her neck by the bedclothes, one bare arm lying outside on the satin quilt. Her fair hair, ashen in the moonlight that fell on her still, pale face, was spread on the pillow, one lock falling across her closed eyes. She did not stir at all as the two men moved cautiously into the room.

"She isn't breathing," Cutfield said, in a whisper, going closer.

"You don't mean—?" in spite of his fear, now almost choking him, Pawley drew nearer himself.

Cutfield felt for a pulse in the slender cold wrist on the satin quilt. He felt nothing. He lifted the hand. It came up with difficulty.

"Stiff," he said. "Cold and stiff and dead these four hours, I reckon."

"Oh, my God!"

9

They stared at each other across the bed. Both were familiar with animal death, in their several trades and in their sport. Both had served at the end of the Second World War and knew human death in more shocking forms than this quiet unblemished corpse presented.

Cutfield took a deep breath and pulled down the bed-clothes. Celia Wainwright was naked, perfect, apparently uninjured in any way. They turned her on her side, they examined her head for any mark of violence under the smooth silken cap of hair. There was none. No blood, no deformity, no sign of violence whatever. A beautiful, un-spoiled body and face, peaceful in death.

They covered her again and looked about the room. Her clothes were piled on a chair, her handbag stood on the dressing table, open. Peering into it by the light of the moon, now getting lower in the sky, they saw a chemist's bottle of capsules, "Poison," Cutfield said, looking at the bottle. "Sleeping things or such-like. Did she take too many herself or were they given her?"

"Young Farnham—" Pawley began and gulped and went on, "—He must have known. He brought her back like this—left her things with her—Now what? The inquest—"

They stared at each other again.

"We don't want—" Cutfield said and turned away.

Pawley said, "You know what they all think—"

"Superstitious lot!" Cutfield burst out, but did not go on.

"All the same," Pawley insisted, "no harm taking pre-cautions. The right precautions." He licked his dry lips and then shrank back suddenly, his face ashen in the moon-light. "She moved! When I said that! I'll swear she moved!"

Cutfield's face, too, was shiny with cold sweat, but he said gruffly, "Be your age! She's dead. You know she's dead."

They stared at the still figure, the smooth white face on the pillow, the spread pale hair behind and round it, the lock fallen again over one eye, hiding perhaps a chink between lid and cheek through which the malevolent, compelling spirit of Celia Wainwright enjoyed the ill-concealed terror of the two men.

With a violent gesture Pawley seized the sheet to pull it up over that face. The stiff arms, both now lying outside, held it down. He struggled, in panic, until Cutfield, cursing him briefly took the arms and forced them underneath the sheet. Both men were breathing heavily as they stood back from the now shrouded form.

"You saw!" the butcher panted. "She resisted that! She struggled!"

"You're bats!" the farmer answered, but without marked conviction.

"So we must—we *must*—"

Cutfield nodded. They looked at their watches. Barely two-thirty. They had four hours, say three and a half. Time enough. Without further discussion they knew what they had to do.

CHAPTER I ·

In May, 1963, a large furniture van drew up in the
lane outside Mulberry Cottage. Dr Frost and his wife, with
smiling faces, walked from the open door to welcome
it.

Henry Frost was a large, white-haired man who looked
older than his sixty years. He had retired from his exhausting
general practice in London in January, having endured the
rigours of the National Health Service for fourteen and a
half years and before that a mixed practice from two years
after the time he had qualified in 1927. He need not have
retired for another five years, but as his colleagues kept reminding him, his pension, for which he had only begun
making contributions in 1948 and which was computed on
Civil Service lines, would be negligible in any case, so why
kill himself over minor ailments and injuries, emergency
calls to children whose parents wanted to shift their responsibility, not to mention endless paper work, for the sake
of a few shillings a year more? Far better to secure now the
compensation money for his former excellent practice that
the Government had bought in and buy himself a place in
the country or a flat in London where he could sit back and
laugh at them all still struggling with the disease-conscious
health-hag-hidden general community.

The argument attracted him. It was possible to succumb
to it when his brother Frank, younger than he, also far
wealthier because he had never married and raised a family,
was killed in an air accident on one of his incessant business
trips abroad. With the exception of a few small legacies
he had left everything to Henry. The legacies were for four

named ladies, no two surnames alike, none of them in any way related to the Frosts, or indeed known to them.

"So much the better," said Mrs Frost. "They aren't likely to quarrel with us over the amounts. Though I must say he doesn't seem to have valued them very highly."

"You jump to improper conclusions far too easily, Jeanie, as I've often told you," her husband said, mildly. "All the same, I anticipate trouble from Aunt Flo."

But there was none, because Aunt Florence, overcome by grief for her favourite nephew, herself died shortly before probate was secured. She had left her estate to Frank and failing him, to Henry.

So there was now no obstacle to retirement and retire Dr Frost did, happy and thankful to lay aside his burden, for though his interest in medicine and human ills was as great as ever, his latter-day drudgery, when all the plums of diagnosis and treatment, all the true emergencies, all the close relationships with whole trusting and respected families had been taken from him, had soured his outlook and frayed both his temper and his endurance.

He was ready to admit, honestly, that the cause lay as much with modern advances in the science of medicine as with the faulty workings of the Health Service. One man alone could not use these advances. He had not the machinery, which needed teams of specialists to apply. He had not the knowledge nor the proliferated skills. But he had missed more and more the exercise of his developed art in treatment and now he was thankful to lay the whole thing on one side and devote himself to interests long suppressed but still latent.

Jean, his wife, insisted upon making their new home in the country, in the south rather than the east or west. The north they did not consider at all, having no ties there of any kind. But in the south their two sons, one a surgeon, the other an engineer, would, with their families, be available for visits. Their daughter, Judy, an occupational therapist at a London hospital, must be able to come to them for weekends. So the south it was, Sussex for preference.

They followed an advertisement to Stourfield and having been directed to Mulberry Cottage at Upfold, fell in love with it and, at a second visit, after a surveyor had reported it sound, bought it outright for a very moderate price.

Of course, as Mr Alford, the estate agent, had pointed out at the first visit, it had been empty for a long time.

"Any particular reason for that?" Dr Frost asked.

Mr Alford seemed a little uneasy but quickly shrugged off the question.

"Bad luck, chiefly." He saw that this was an ambiguous answer, likely to be misconstrued. "What I mean is, the owner had bad luck with his first tenants. Oh yes, it was let to begin with."

"How long for?" Mrs Frost asked.

"Three years, madam. We didn't handle it ourselves. Mr Wainwright made the arrangements with some friends of his, I believe. They were not used to the country. They left, as I said, after three years. It was then Mr Wainwright put the property in our hands to sell. We thought there'd be no trouble as it's so attractive. Don't you agree?"

He beat up his flagging salesmanship. It was clear to the Frosts that he was without hope, driven by despair and weariness to utter honesty.

"I think it's a lovely house," Mrs Frost said, unexpectedly. "Don't you, Harry?"

Dr Frost recognised that this was where he would spend his declining years, so he said cautiously, "Well, I don't know. It'll need a hell of a lot doing to it."

"Naturally, after so long," his wife agreed, knowing she had won. "That's why the price is so reasonable. Isn't it, Mr Alford?"

"The price couldn't be lower," he answered, truthfully. It had reached rock-bottom, where his profits were negligible, his work over the years mostly wasted. His only desire now was to get the place off his books. 'The Deadly Mulberry' was what they called it in the office and no wonder.

"It'll have to be re-decorated throughout," said Dr Frost.

"It's stood up to last winter simply marvellously," Mrs Frost replied. "No bursts, no broken windows—"

"That's usually hooligans. And the tanks will have been empty for years." He looked inquiringly at Mr Alford.

"Yes, sir. We don't have much trouble from hooligans hereabouts. The boys shoot birds, mostly—or one another sometimes. Not at windows."

"That's a blessing. The garden is a complete mess, of course."

"Which is just what you wanted," Mrs Frost reminded him. "You're longing to get at it and re-design the whole thing."

"Perhaps I am," he admitted.

They stood side by side and hand in hand in the new grass springing from the lumpy field that had been a lawn. They looked at the mulberry tree and the view beyond the hedge and back at the mellow house behind them.

"Well, what about it?" Dr Frost asked, knowing the answer. She squeezed his hand, not bothering to make it.

So Mr Alford, surprised into unusual smiles and enthusiasm, went back in the Frosts' car to Stourfield, to begin negotiations with Mr Wainwright's solicitors.

"He's a very old gentleman," he said and added vaguely, "But I don't anticipate any undue delay. May I put you in touch with a builder for the alterations?"

"Decorations," Mrs Frost corrected. "There won't be any alterations, will there, Harry?"

"The kitchen—central heating?" suggested Mr Alford.

"I shall have the place surveyed as the next step," Dr Frost said, recalling the others from their flights of fancy. "If that's satisfactory I agree to the terms. Want a deposit?"

"It would be desirable, sir," said Mr Alford, "in case of other prospective buyers."

He was quite carried away by the afternoon's success and was only recalled by the gleam of amusement in the doctor's eyes, which made him blush in spite of his years and experience.

So the survey was made and a local builder, Snowthorne, put in charge of the decorations. And two months later, in May, the furniture van drew up at the house and Dr Frost, who had been waiting in the hall, called out, "Here they are, Jeanie," and Mrs Frost ran from the kitchen and together they went out to welcome their possessions to their new home.

The cockney removal men worked with a will. They had cleared up Dr Frost's London house the day before and regarding him as a fellow native of the city were prepared to indulge this curious whim of his to bury himself in the wilds. They approved of the new decorations on the whole, though they would have preferred more pastel shades on the walls and a more lavish display of modern kitchen equipment. In their own homes these points had been attended to. The driver had a suburban garden too, and shook his head over the state of the Mulberry lawn and flower beds.

"Want it re-designed for a start," he suggested to the doctor. "Cut down on the work. Paving and that. Shrubs. Get rid of that old tree for a start."

"God forbid!" said Dr Frost, laughing. "I'd have to find a new name for the place if I did that."

"See wot you mean," the man answered, grinding his cigarette end with his heel into the path near the gate.

They had just knocked off for their morning break when a car drew up behind the great van and Mr Snowthorne got out, followed by his wife. She was a fresh-faced woman with a kindly smile. Leaving her husband to speak to the doctor she made her way into the house to find Mrs Frost.

"You'll excuse me barging in," she said, in her pleasant country voice. "I'm Mrs Snowthorne. My hubby wanted a word with the doctor, so I came along to say I've got a thermos of coffee in the car if you'd care to share it with us."

"How very kind of you," Mrs Frost answered gratefully. It seemed a long time already since they had hurried through their hotel breakfast in Stourfield and though much of their furniture had already been placed in the various rooms the men had done no more for the kitchen than dump into it three large nailed-up packing cases of china and glass.

"You'd best come out to the car, then," said Mrs Snowthorn. "Rest your feet. I know what these removals are. Nearly kill you."

They sat in the back of the builder's roomy Vauxhall. Mrs Snowthorne had offered to get their picnic table and chairs out of the boot, but neither woman cared for the prospect of setting them up on the rough uneven lawn with its long grass wet from showers in the night.

Mrs Frost found her hostess most helpful. Mrs Snowthorne enjoyed telling the new arrival about shops in the village and in Stourfield, about what she could get in Upfold and more important, what she could not get there. Mrs Frost learned the names of the vicar, the doctor and other persons of importance in the neighbourhood, including Farmer Cutfield, who had a young brother studying to be a doctor.

"*Is* a doctor," Mrs Snowthorne corrected herself. "He's been qualified for above a year. Working at St Edmund's Hospital in London."

"That's my husband's old hospital," Mrs Frost exclaimed. Mrs Snowthorne was delighted.

The two men came up to the car; more cups were produced from the fitted picnic basket. Mrs Frost, feeling rested, got out into the fresh air again, enjoying every minute of this clear May morning, with no telephone calls to send her hurrying indoors, no verbal messages to be sorted out with difficulty from a stream of irrelevant comment, no demands for visits, for prescription renewals, for advice on totally unmedical subjects; on this day no shopping, no cooking, no keeping a meal hot long after it was spoiled; in the future, no night calls, no emergencies, hardly any more responsibility at all.

"You'll be much in demand, doctor," she heard Mrs Snowthorne saying. "I don't doubt they'll be putting you up for the U.D.C. before you know where you are."

"And we know who'll be round in two twos to get Mrs Frost lined up," said Mr Snowthorne, taking this cue. "Mrs Graveney."

They both laughed. The Frosts looked at them in dismay.

"Mrs Graveney's the W.I.," they were told.

"Oh, I see," said Mrs Frost, weakly. To change the now rather alarming prospect before them she began to ask questions about the former owner of the cottage.

"I don't mean the people who had it for the first three years after Mr Wainwright left. I mean why did he go away? He was quite elderly at the time. I mean, according to Mr Alford he's really old now, over seventy, so he must have been over sixty then."

As she was saying all this Mrs Frost did not notice, as her husband did, the growing embarrassment on the faces of the builder and his wife. But she could not fail to notice the long silence that followed. She looked from one to the other, then, astonished that her words should produce such an effect, she added, "Have I said anything I shouldn't?"

"Oh no," Mr Snowthorne hastened to assure her and Mrs Snowthorne murmured in a low voice, "It was after he lost his wife."

Mrs Frost wanted to ask the obvious next question as to why and how she had died or been lost, which should, but did not always mean the same thing. But Mr Snowthorne said in a hearty voice, "Well, mother, we'd best be getting on. The doctor and Mrs Frost are needed back in the house, I see."

In fact one of the removal men, with a sofa on his back, was teetering on the doorstep, looking back briefly for guidance before dumping it in the first room he came to.

"Oh, dear me!" Mrs Frost said. "I must show him."

She shook Mrs Snowthorne's hand, thanked her warmly for the coffee and advice and hurried away. The Snowthornes climbed back into the car and drove off. Halfway to their home Mr Snowthorne said, "She wasn't satisfied. Nor was he."

"Well, I can't help their curiosity," his wife answered. "I couldn't put it anyways else, could I? Nobody could. They'll find that out soon enough."

By mid-afternoon the van was empty. After tea, produced by Mrs Frost, who now had quite a number of implements and utensils unpacked in the kitchen, the men went on their way again, leaving a trail of shavings, newspaper, cigarette ends and cartons of various sizes all the way from the front door to the gate. Inside the house there was a semblance of order, with carpets laid and the heavy pieces of furniture in their right places. These last actions had been a favour, not always granted, but offered on this occasion out of a genuine, warm-hearted respect for Dr Frost's age and profession.

The couple went slowly back into the house after the van had disappeared down the road.

"Sit down, Jeanie," Dr Frost said. "I'm going to find us a drink and after that we'll go back to the hotel for dinner. I reserved us a table there this morning."

"Oh, Harry," Mrs Frost answered. "That was wonderful of you." But she would not sit down. "While you dig out the sherry," she said, "I'll just go up and make the beds. I've got the sheets and blankets out already."

"You're far more of a wonder than I am," he said, fondly. When he kissed her, she thought to herself, "What have I done to be such a lucky woman?" But she did not say it aloud because she knew what his answer would be.

At dinner in the hotel at Stourfield they compared their several conversations with the Snowthornes.

"Very decent of them to come along this morning," Dr Frost said. "Actually I had mentioned one or two things I wanted altered in the garage, but he needn't have brought his wife and made such an occasion of it. Very pleasant and welcoming. The business side was trivial from his point of view."

"I liked her," Mrs Frost answered. "Just the sort of genuine, unpretentious countrywoman you hope they'll all be. I think we're going to like Upfold. Oh and she told me one very useful thing. She knows a daily who may be able to give me two mornings a week. A Mrs Thompson. Lives in the village. A widow. Used to work for the Wainwrights and also the early tenants. Her daughter got married recently and left home, so she has more time on her hands."

"Won't she be a bit long in the tooth? It's ten years since the Wainwrights left."

"I asked that at once. She was left a widow quite young, in the war. Two young children, I think Mrs Snowthorne said. I shall go and see her tomorrow. Mrs S. said she'd have a word with her tonight if she was in. So she may come up to see me—Mrs. Thompson, I mean."

"Snowthorne made a point of being helpful, too," Dr Frost said. "He offered to put me in touch with the Wainwrights' gardener."

Mrs Frost laughed.

"You'd think they'd all been in a state of suspended animation since Mulberry Cottage fell empty. What did you say?"

"Oh, thanked him and said I proposed to occupy myself getting it into order again. Must have exercise and an object and that sort of thing. He looked at me as if I'd gone out of my mind. He's more of an urban type than his wife. She's a connection of a farmer at Upfold. Man called Cutfield."

"So that was why she told me about young Cutfield, the brother. Medical. St Edmund's."

"Really? I'll have to look him up."

The Frosts drove back to the house in a very mellow, satisfied frame of mind. The removal could not have gone off more smoothly. Tomorrow and for several days to come they would have a delicious time arranging their possessions, the books, the ornaments, the pictures, the smaller pieces of furniture. And there was absolutely no hurry. None of it had to be done in time snatched from a compelling duty. That was bliss in itself. A full reward for duty done.

In this smug mood the doctor locked up the garage and decided to walk once round his property before going indoors.

He was a little surprised to see footprints in the grass and on the dew-damp stone flags near the kitchen door. They led to the coal-shed, but the removal men had not been near the coal-shed. At any rate, not after the dew had fallen.

He shrugged his shoulders. The village lads were naturally curious, he thought. All the same, he was glad he had locked up the house before going in to Stourfield.

When he followed his wife upstairs, later, she called him into her bedroom. Hers was at the front of the house, his at the back.

"Look at that," she said, pointing to the bed.

He leaned over the pillow. There was a light sprinkling of some crumbly greyish material on it. He looked at the wall behind the bed, at the ceiling above.

"It looks like plaster," he said. "But I can't see where it's fallen from."

"Nor can I. Funny, isn't it? It wasn't there when I made the bed. I mean, there wasn't any on the bed *before* I made it."

"Sure?"

"Quite sure."

He thought he would not tell her about the prowler he decided had been round the house while they were out.

22

Could the chap have got in? Quite easily, of course, by the coal-shed roof and the bathroom window. They had left all the upstairs windows open, to air the bedrooms. Plaster —or dust? From a hand? A foot? An animal, possibly? A cat? Too vague—too unlikely. Where from, then?

He gave it up. The prowler had done no harm, obviously. Curiosity about newcomers would not last. But he would remember in future to fasten the windows, particularly the bathroom window, as well as the doors when the house was going to be empty, and he would keep that bathroom window shut every night, too.

CHAPTER II

The Frosts found the rest of the Upfold people just as welcoming and easy to get on with as the Snowthornes had been on the day of their arrival.

"We might have lived here all our lives," Mrs Frost told her London friends, when they drove down, as they very soon did, to see how she and Harry were getting on. And indeed she was made to feel at home, not only by the owners of the small row of village shops in the High Street, but also by a growing number of retired and commuting families in the neighbourhood.

Prominent among these was Mrs Graveney. Mrs Frost recognised her from Mrs Snowthorne's description when she went into the general store on the morning after the removal.

Mrs Graveney was buying stamps at the Post Office counter of the store. She gave Mrs Frost a sharp look, hovered while the latter in her turn asked for stamps and apparently satisfied by the newcomer's manner of speaking and general appearance, moved away. On the following day they found themselves together in Mr Pawley's shop, buying meat. Mrs Graveney flashed a very toothy smile at Mrs Frost and said, "I believe you have come to Mulberry Cottage, haven't you?"

"Yes," Mrs Frost answered. "We moved in the day before yesterday."

"So wise of you to shop locally at once," said Mrs Graveney in a low voice, "even if later on you go into Stourfield for most things."

As Mr Pawley now returned from the back of his shop, where he had been cutting off a joint for Mrs Graveney, she added in a louder voice, "You'll find the meat here quite excellent, Mrs—er—"

"Frost," said the latter.

Mrs Graveney turned her attention to the joint in Pawley's hand, approved it, asked for it to be sent up and without paying for it, prepared to leave the shop. Before she went she said to Mrs Frost, "We never pay calls now-a-days, do we? But won't you come and have tea with me one day? You and the doctor, too, I mean?"

"We should like to very much," said Mrs Frost, politely. She was not sure what Harry would say nor was she in the least attracted by Mrs Graveney, but she foresaw many similar situations of this nature which would have to be endured before they found their own circle in Upfold.

"What about tomorrow?" said Mrs Graveney.

"If Harry hasn't made any other plans for tomorrow, yes, thank you," said Mrs Frost, applying a formula she had used for over thirty years.

Mrs Graveney smiled again, told Mrs Frost not to bother to ring up if they could come and left the shop. Mrs Frost turned her attention to her own joint and found Pawley extremely helpful and rather more expensive than the big self-service store she had used in London. Later, when Harry said the meat was the best he had tasted for years, she decided to continue with Pawley for the present. If, when she was

24

no longer a new customer, the quality and service went off, she would look for a branch of her former store in Stourfield.

"It's so wonderful not having to carry everything home," she said. "It takes one back to before the war."

Dr Frost laughed.

"Considering you parked the car practically outside Pawley's shop, I don't see that that applies."

"Parking," Mrs Frost said, with a sigh of added pleasure. "Yes, no more parking trouble. No driving round to find a place for half an hour, no meters, no full-up parks. Just a nice little set of white lines, half of them empty."

"You wait till the weekend," Dr Frost suggested.

They went to tea with Mrs Graveney the next day. The exaggerated thatch that had already made them laugh when they passed the house on their way into the village, was matched by the interior, where huge low-placed beams, performing no very obvious function, menaced Dr Frost's head both in the hall and in the large drawing-room.

A girl in a flowered overall brought tea. The Frosts answered a good many questions about their life in London, the practice there, the children and their careers.

"We have only one son," Mrs Graveney said. "He's representing my husband's firm in Mexico at present."

This was clearly intended to start the Frosts on a reciprocal set of questions, but as neither of them was in the least interested in Mr Graveney's business activities, the success of which was only too obvious all about them, the conversation began to languish.

In order to revive it Mrs Frost asked, "Have you lived here long?"

"Nearly fifteen years," Mrs Graveney answered. "Terrible, isn't it?"

"Why?" Dr Frost asked. "I mean, why terrible? It seems to me a charming place."

He meant the village, but Mrs Graveney took his remark to refer to her house and was flattered.

25

"I'm so glad you think so. It isn't everyone who likes thatch. The insurers for one." She paused for the accustomed laugh, but not getting it, went on. "You see, we wanted to feel really rural and now, I believe, it's rather fashionable to have thatch, so we were being quite avant-garde, weren't we?"

Dr Frost did not bother to put things straight. His wife said, "Fifteen years. Then you will have known the Wainwrights."

Mrs Graveney's face changed. It became both serious and eager. She leaned a little forward.

"Oh yes," she said. "I knew the Wainwrights."

Mrs Frost was puzzled. Dr Frost sighed. He knew the signs. This was how patients had looked and spoken when they had some, to them, mysterious ailment to describe.

Mrs Frost asked, "Were they here when you came?"

"Oh, no. There was an old lady living at Mulberry Cottage then. A relation of the Singletons. They are our local bigwigs, you know. She died and then Mr Wainwright bought it. He used it only at weekends at first. After he married Celia he was here most of the time. At least he always went to London on Tuesday morning and came back on Thursday evening."

"I gather he was getting on in years when he was here," Dr Frost said. "His wife the same, I suppose?"

"We were told he went away when she died," Mrs Frost explained.

"Who told you that?" Mrs Graveney had become very red in the face. With her heavy make-up the effect was quite startling. Without waiting for an answer she went on, in an excited voice, "Celia was anything but old. A lovely girl, not more than twenty-five, I shouldn't think. When he first brought her down we all thought she was his daughter, or a niece, possibly. He never spoke about his family. He wasn't very sociable."

The Frosts nodded. Clearly Mr Wainwright had resisted

Mrs Graveney. He had been more strong-minded than themselves. Or perhaps he had never really wished to make a home at Upfold, as they did. He was a weekender, Mrs Graveney had said.

"But she died?" Dr Frost persisted, mildly.

Mrs Graveney was getting annoyed.

"If she did, it wasn't in Upfold," she declared, almost rudely. "She left. That's all I know. My husband and I were away on holiday at the time. She was here when we went off, and there was no suggestion then that she might be leaving. She'd gone when we came back. Julian—you won't have met him yet—Julian Farnham—"

"The author, Julian Farnham?" asked Dr Frost.

"That's the one. He knew her—well. We expected him to tell us—he was really a great friend of hers—but he was still on holiday when we came back."

"And afterwards?"

"He would never speak about her. Turned the conversation at once."

"How odd," Mrs Frost said. "In a village everyone knows about everyone else. Or so one is told."

"The village!" Mrs Graveney's mouth took on a pinched look. "They know all right. But where Celia's concerned you'd never get a word out of them for love or money."

"Why?"

Mrs Graveney's face changed. She got up briskly.

"If you'll excuse me I'll just take the tray out to Betty, so she can wash up before she goes. Then perhaps you'd like to see my garden. The azaleas are really lovely this year."

A few days later Mrs Frost received a visit from the vicar. The Reverend Maurice Shalford knew, as all Upfold knew, from the moment the faded 'For Sale' notice on its rickety time-worn post was covered with a fresh sticker proclaiming 'Sold' in bright red letters, that there would be strangers in the village. He expected, or rather he hoped, to see them at church three days after their arrival. He intended to greet them on their way out, welcome them, introduce them to his wife and to one or two of their friends and invite them to take a glass of sherry at the vicarage before they went home to their lunch.

But the Frosts did not appear at matins and one of Mr Shalford's friends told him he had seen Dr Frost in his garden hacking away at one of the overgrown borders. The vicar expressed Christian understanding and went round to Mulberry Cottage on Tuesday morning.

He was welcomed into the house by Mrs Frost. The doctor had gone to London for the day, she told him. She would be meeting him with the car at Stourfield railway station in the evening.

"I have been remiss," said the vicar. "I should have called last week. But I thought you might be in church on Sunday."

Mrs Frost was amused. Mr Shalford assumed that they were Church of England Christians simply because they had come to live at Mulberry Cottage and Harry was a doctor. She wondered what the vicar would do or say if she said they were Buddhists or Moslems or even some brand of English non-conformist. But she restrained herself and simply told him the truth, which was that on Sunday they had still been very busy getting the books finally arranged and making a start on the garden.

"We're not regular church-goers," she said, with mild deceit. "Medical practice is busier than ever, you know, on Sunday. No regular surgeries, but people usually come up to plead they had no time on weekdays. Harry was too indulgent, I'm afraid. But he began to practice in the days when the G.P. was a friend and adviser all round, not just a technician or sorting house."

It was a test speech. The vicar recognised it as such. He rose to the occasion.

"Your husband, Mrs Frost, was doing God's business better that way than on his knees in church."

28

Mrs Frost liked the ringing tones of Mr Shalford's beautiful voice as he said these words, so she had not the heart to tell him her husband was an agnostic. Instead she murmured a few words about looking forward to seeing the church and offered the vicar a cup of mid-morning coffee, which he accepted with pleasure.

While she was getting it he wandered over to the book shelves that lined three walls of the sitting-room and shook his head a little over some of the titles he found amongst the fiction. The more serious reading matter included much that was familiar and some that he made up his mind to borrow later on.

Over the coffee Mrs Frost brought the conversation round to the Wainwrights. Mrs Graveney's evasiveness had made her curious.

"The Wainwrights were rather birds of passage, I gather?" she said.

"Who told you that?"

Again the cautious approach, the following question.

"Mrs Graveney. I understand from her that Mr Wainwright used this house for weekends until he married. And then was in London for the middle of each week."

"Yes. Yes, it's true they were only here for a few years. I forget—"

He broke off; very obviously he found this topic distasteful.

"Mrs Graveney was very vague," Mrs Frost pursued. "So was someone else who spoke about it. Mr Wainwright gave up the house after his wife had—*gone*, they all say. Does this mean she died—or that she left him?"

Mr Shalford put a hand to his head.

"I'm sorry," Mrs Frost said. "I've no right to be inquisitive. They were friends of yours? How dreadful of me!"

"No, no!" Mr Shalford protested. "I can see what is happening. Not for the first time, alas! You had better hear it from me. Rather than from—others."

"Hear *what*?" exclaimed Mrs Frost, now quite frightened.

"She disappeared," said Mr Shalford. "Between one day and the next she—*disappeared*."

Mrs Frost was puzzled.

"You mean—she went away from Upfold?"

"I suppose so."

The vicar looked at her with unhappy eyes.

"You may have heard of the discrepancy in their ages. Celia, Mrs Wainwright, was twenty-five when she came here. He must have been over sixty."

Mrs Frost nodded.

"Yes. I gather from what my husband says that he's well over seventy now."

"He looked much younger than sixty," the vicar went on. "He was devoted to her. She was so young and so pretty and so gentle. She was very much admired—at first."

"And then?"

"I should not be telling you this," Mr Shalford went on. "But as a doctor's wife you will have come across strange things in your time. The village people grew to fear her and that led to dislike—even *hate*."

His voice dropped as he spoke. He went on hurriedly.

"I am telling you this principally because my wife tells me you are employing Mrs Thompson."

"Yes. She says she will give me two mornings a week, starting tomorrow. Wednesdays and Saturdays. Of course," she added, remembering, "Mrs Shalford has her on Tuesdays and Thursdays, doesn't she?"

Mr Shalford smiled, handed over his cup and got up to go. At the door he held Mrs Frost's hand for a moment as he said, "Well, it has been a great pleasure to meet you. I hope now that you have more time you will find you can come to church now and then. Our congregation is not large—"

He spoke wistfully, looking back at less godless times when his predecessor's services had been thronged.

"Young people with their cars and motorbikes—Stourfield

30

is no distance from us, now." He paused, seemed to check himself, to recollect. Then he leaned towards her and said earnestly, "I think she went away that night because she could no longer bear to live with us here. On the one side —love—on the other—hate."

"But—but did you never hear where she went? People *can't* disappear. Mr Wainwright—"

The vicar shook his head.

"I don't know. When he came back and found her gone— He did not come to me. He saw Dr Marshall. Then he went away and he never came back."

"Never at all?"

"No. Alford was put in charge. Wainwright never came to Upfold again."

"So he must have found her, mustn't he? I mean—unless she'd just left him and he had to let her go. There wasn't anything in the papers, was there? No divorce, or anything?"

Mrs Frost's imagination was running away with her. The vicar brought her back.

"As far as we know," he said, gravely, "there was nothing to go in the papers. But we never speak of it, here, now."

This was as much a command as a statement and Mrs Frost took it as such.

When she met the train at Stourfield that evening her mind was still full of the curious history of the Wainwrights' departure from Upfold. But Dr Frost wanted to tell her about his day in London which he did on the drive home and when they arrived there they saw a farm jeep standing near their gate, with a breeched and gaitered figure standing beside it, looking over the hedge into their garden.

"You go and talk to him," Mrs Frost said. "I'll go in the back way and get our supper on the table."

But when she carried the first tray into the dining-room she found her husband stooping over the cupboard in the sideboard.

"It's Cutfield," he explained. "Farmer chap with a brother

31

at St Edmund's. I've asked him in. Must give him a drink. Come and join us."

The farmer was a pleasant change from poor ineffectual Mr Shalford, Mrs Frost thought, looking at him as she shook hands. In his middle thirties, strong, brown-faced, with a pleasant country voice and a positive manner.

"You must help me, Mrs Frost," he began at once. "I'm trying to persuade the doctor to keep a few hens. I've got a lovely lot of Leghorn, crossed Rhode Island. I'll bring them on for you and you can have them later in the summer, for laying in the autumn. Give you plenty of eggs and broilers for the table when they go off lay and you get replacements. Nothing like free-run birds to give you an egg with the real taste. Use up all your scraps, too."

Dr Frost laughed heartily.

"Don't listen to his sales talk, Jeanie," he said. "I've refused the kind offer already, though I've booked several yards of manure to put into this poor starved garden."

"But it's Mrs Frost'd look after them," the farmer said. "The lady always runs the poultry. What about it, Mrs Frost? The old hen-house is still at the bottom of the garden, see."

"It won't be after tomorrow," Dr Frost said. "Snowthorne's taking it down to make way for a new toolshed."

"I'm sorry, Mr Cutfield," Mrs Frost assured him. "I'm afraid I don't know the first thing about keeping hens and I'm too old to learn. Besides, Harry has his plans all fixed for the garden and after the way I've bullied him about the inside of the house I wouldn't dare lay down the law over the outside."

They all laughed and the question of the hens was dropped and not revived. Instead the conversation turned to the younger Cutfield and to St Edmund's Hospital and the prospects for clever young men in the medical profession today. After he had finished his drink Cutfield went on his way with a promise to let the doctor know when his brother would be in Upfold, so that the two generations of St Edmund's men could meet and compare notes.

When the Frosts sat down at last to their supper Mrs Frost said, "Our vicar called this morning. He was kind and pleasant as everyone is here, even the extraordinary Mrs Graveney. He has a beautiful voice. But he said some very odd things about the Wainwrights."

"Such as?"

She told him.

CHAPTER III

Before the end of the week Dr Frost paid a call on the local general practitioner, Dr Marshall. This was partly a courtesy visit from a medical newcomer to the district, though it had no real significance as such, since Dr Frost was no longer in practice. He wanted to visit Dr Marshall chiefly in order to meet one who might attend him in his old age.

Dr Frost arranged to reach the doctor's house about the time a normal morning surgery in London would end. He discovered that Dr Marshall saw very few people at his own house and those by appointment, mostly in the evenings. Dr Frost was on the point of making such an appointment when the doctor appeared.

"I'll come again," the former said. "I was just making a date—"

"Indeed you won't," Dr Marshall said. "Come in now and share my coffee break. I usually drop in for it about now and to collect the late visits that people won't ring up for early enough."

"Don't I know," answered Dr Frost, following the younger man into the house.

He was introduced to Mrs Marshall, who brought a tray to the surgery and then left the two men together.

Dr Frost produced National Health cards.

"For myself and my wife," he said, "if you'll take us on."

"I don't need those," Dr Marshall answered. "Only too pleased—"

But Dr Frost insisted.

"Professional etiquette is all right in its way," he said, "and in its day. I know you'd treat us for nothing, but there's no point in making presents to the Government. As you see, we were on a list in London, my junior partner's, as a matter of fact, so I actually benefited as well as he."

They both laughed and Dr Marshall, accepting the cards, put them away in a drawer of his table.

"We won't trouble you much. At the start, anyway," Dr Frost said, concluding that part of his visit.

They chatted amiably for a time, chiefly about the difference between London and country practice and the continuing frustrations and faults of the Health Service. Dr Frost learned that Dr Marshall had lived in Upfold for nearly fifteen years; that he had begun general practice two years after he qualified and had taken a job as trainee assistant to a large group of doctors in Stourfield before becoming a partner in the firm.

"We practically run the town and the neighbourhood," he said. "There are only two other firms and a solo chap who fancies himself as a psychiatrist and takes all the crackpots off our hands."

"Sounds ideal," said Dr Frost.

"Except that the border line crackpots are mostly private patients with money."

Dr Frost nodded.

"The kind I hung on to like grim death in the old days. Kept them out of lunatic asylums and made a very steady income out of them. Satisfactory to all concerned."

34

"Treatment being what it was then. Now they more or less *have* to get their treatment at a hospital."

"Oh, quite."

This exchange led on to a further discussion of eccentrics, illustrated with anecdote, where Dr Frost had the advantage. With a little careful handling he saw that he could introduce the Wainwrights and did so, with gratifying results.

To begin with Dr Marshall's whole demeanour changed when Dr Frost introduced the name. But the latter continued to remark upon various aspects of the Wainwright ownership of Mulberry Cottage. These had genuinely intrigued him from the first.

"There's nothing wrong with the house, is there?" he said. "I mean, we find it so attractive and our survey was exceptionally good, no damp, no dry rot and so on. Yet the old boy himself seems to have been here for no more than three or four years altogether and some friends of his for an equally short time, and until we came on the scene the place was empty for the best part of seven years."

Dr Marshall did not answer directly. He merely said, "But you know why he went away?"

"Not really. His wife left him, I believe. My wife gathered the bare facts from the vicar, but got no details. I suppose one wouldn't expect her to, from that source. Anyway we aren't keen on gossip or looking for scandal. But I would rather like to know what happened. These days you don't expect to find the sort of reticence, discomfort, embarrassment —even a sort of fear—that we've met in connection with what seems to be a sad, but fairly commonplace event."

"Sad, yes, very," answered Dr Marshall. His face was filled with a kind of heavy grief that supported all Dr Frost's bewilderment. "Celia Wainwright was a patient of mine," he added.

This was a plain way of saying he did not propose to answer any direct questions about her, Dr Frost decided. But it was also a very subtle, not unusual way of informing him that here had been some definite medical aspects of the case which could be fairly obvious. Dr Marshall's next guarded words confirmed this view.

"She was less than half his age," he said. "She was quite lovely to look at."

He glanced at his watch. Dr Frost rose at once.

"I mustn't keep you," he said. "D'you know, just at this moment I could almost envy you. For the first time since I retired."

Dr Marshall smiled. He was inclined to like the old man. But he felt the pressure of his work and saw nothing in particular about it to envy.

"You must meet my partners," he said as they moved to the door. "Two of them live in Stourfield, where we have the group surgery. Our present assistant lives over it. The fourth is out on the other side."

Dr Frost thanked him and walked away, while Dr Marshall went back into the house to collect names and addresses and organise the rest of the morning visits.

"Well, did you get anything out of him about the Wainrights?" Mrs Frost asked at lunch.

"I did not. She was a patient of his. He mentioned the difference in their ages."

"So does everyone. What they don't say, which is so very odd these days, is who she ran away with that night."

"Aren't you jumping to conclusions?"

"Haven't you jumped already?"

"Well, yes, I suppose so. It's only sex that people in this country would be so mysterious over."

"Exactly. But less so now than ten years ago."

"Perhaps not in the country."

"I wonder. It seems to me there must be more to it than just an elopement. Even Mrs Graveney said practically nothing. She'd be the first to relay an ordinary romance."

"Even an adulterous one?"

36

"Certainly. She'd revel in it. Besides. Oh, Harry, he was old enough to be her father!"

"But he wasn't her father. He was her husband."

"Old men can be very foolish."

"And young women very greedy. She need not have married him. By all accounts she should have had no difficulty in marrying a man of her own age."

"There must have been something odd about her, I suppose. Or about him."

"About them both, perhaps."

During the next two weeks Mrs Frost heard a number of things that seemed both to her and the doctor to be not only odd, but sinister and tragic as well.

The information came from the daily cleaner, Mrs Thompson, who had been working at Mulberry Cottage ten years ago for the Wainwrights and then for their immediate successors.

Mrs Thompson was a small, thin woman with a lined face and an expression of unalterable gloom. She spoke seldom; when she did she spoke through her teeth, with a mixture of rage and bitterness quite out of keeping with the words she uttered. Mrs Frost was startled at first but grew used to it.

Dr Frost on the other hand diagnosed a gastric neurosis brought on by the hard life she had lived as a war widow, but when Mrs Frost told him that, on the contrary, Mrs Thompson ate heartily and with no apparent misgivings at the mid-morning break, he revised this opinion.

"She's just permanently unhappy, I think," Mrs Frost told him. "I expect she'll tell me why when we get to know each other better."

In the meantime, since the Frosts, with their experience, realised that their new daily was not a person who responded to questioning, they gave her friendliness and consideration and patient understanding. They were soon rewarded.

Mrs Thompson was upstairs in Mrs Frost's bedroom when the latter, who was cleaning the glass shelf in the bathroom, heard a crash. She hurried out on to the landing. Mrs Thompson appeared in the doorway of the bedroom carrying a photograph frame and a handful of glass fragments.

"I'm ever so sorry," she said, the rage in her voice accentuated. "It slipped out of me hand."

"Never mind," Mrs Frost answered. "The photo isn't scratched a bit. It's my son," she explained, "only of course he's much older than that, now. He was eighteen when that was taken. His first term at Cambridge. He's the eldest of my family."

"I guessed that," Mrs Thompson said. "I was looking at it and thinking my Roy'd been going on for thirty if he'd lived—" Her voice broke and when she spoke again, came very differently, on a high note now, full of pride and love and desperate sorrow. "My Roy was ever such a bright little lad. His sisters weren't a patch on him—still aren't. He got in the grammar at Stourfield and they were putting him in for a university scholarship. They gave me a grant at sixteen so I could keep him on into the sixth form. I lost their father in the war."

"Yes, I heard that," Mrs Frost said. "You must have had a hard struggle."

"It was well worth it. Roy was worth every bit of it. Till *she* came here."

"You mean—you mean—?"

Mrs Thompson's face was changing into a mask of terror and hatred. She nodded.

"No need to mention the name. None of us care to utter it. Diabolical. She murdered my boy, Mrs Frost."

"Oh, *no*!"

The doctor's wife was profoundly shocked; appalled, too, to realise that she was accepting the daily's statement. She rallied her common sense.

"You can't mean that, literally. That she actually killed— That you know it—But nothing was *done*—she was not—"

"She was responsible. Roy passed this house every day on his bike going in to school. His last term she began it."

38

"Began *what*?"

"She spelled him," Mrs Thompson said. Her voice had gone back to its normal tone which did nothing to reassure Mrs Frost. "Put a spell on him. He changed before my very eyes."

"You mean, don't you, that he unfortunately fell in love with her?"

"It was more than that. Boys get a crush on a girl. Roy took up with one and another—he'd known them from a little chap. He wasn't old enough to have a steady. This was different. I didn't realise at the time. Thought it was the exam was worrying him."

"I expect it was. It was very important to him, wasn't it?"

"He had no thought for the exam. Only for her. I found that out afterwards. He'd be late for school because he'd waited to see her go out to feed her chickens when he passed. He'd be late home, waiting to catch another glimpse."

"Wasn't it just calf love? Boys sometimes take it very hard."

Mrs Thompson shook her head.

"She encouraged him. She used her wicked power. We know she had it. Roy was always up in arms on her side. Over the other things. He called me superstitious to my face once. She had him all right."

"But she went away," Mrs Frost said, shrinking from what she knew must come.

"Too late," said Mrs Thompson. "Roy hanged himself. They said at the inquest it was through failing in the exam. But that was on account of her, too. As I very well knew."

"It's a wicked world!" cried Mrs Frost, in despair at such cruel circumstance.

"She was a wicked woman," said Mrs Thompson, turning away into the bedroom.

"Was?"

"I reckon the devil, her master, has her now," said the bitter voice from inside the room.

Later that day Mrs Frost told her husband the story. Without the overtones supplied by Mrs Thompson it seemed a familiar sad tale of pressure and failure and their consequences in destructive power on a young, not very robust, mind and character.

"I suppose that's really all there was to it," Mrs Frost said, with a sigh. "Nothing to do with Mrs Wainwright, really."

"Oh, I didn't say that," Dr Frost corrected her. "The boy may very well have been infatuated. Especially if she went out of her way to be kind to him and gave him a friendly word now and then. The infatuation would be likely to spoil his concentration on his school work and wreck the exam. Then, finding he'd failed he'd realise what an ass he'd been to ditch himself for a woman. Not an unusual situation at all. But I'd have thought he might have used it as an excuse to himself. At that age I wouldn't really expect—"

"You mean he wasn't humiliated by finding his ability inferior?"

"Exactly. Only that he'd been distracted at the wrong moment."

"Then there must have been something else. Something to do with her, directly?"

They looked at each other in silence. At last Dr Frost said, "We don't really know anything about her, do we? After all, poor Mrs Thompson has to put the blame on someone. Chiefly because she didn't realise what was happening to the boy."

"And was consumed by her ambition for his future. I suppose that's it," Mrs Frost said again.

But she was not satisfied and as the days passed she found that the village people took every opportunity they could to tell her things about Mrs Wainwright, none of them to her credit and some of them of an extremely frightening nature.

The man who called for the laundry, for instance. He was the husband of a Mrs Winter, who took in a limited amount of washing. He called to offer his wife's services a few days after the Frosts' arrival, explaining that Mulberry Cottage was on his normal route to and from his work and he would be happy to oblige.

Mrs Frost accepted the offer. On Mr Winter's third appearance he congratulated her upon not having a dog to bite strangers.

"Those Wainwrights," he said. "It was her, really. You'd hear her call the brute inside and you'd see nothing of it till you were leaving. Then like as not it'd spring out and nip you. She'd do that a purpose."

"The dog, you mean?" Mrs Frost suggested.

"Oh no, the lady. One of her tricks. Like sending the dog after Cutfield's sheep."

"Surely not!"

"It's a fact. He had a lot of trouble that way. A whole lot savaged—dropped their lambs—two dead and another had to be destroyed. It went on, off and on, for months."

"But why didn't the Wainwrights get rid of the dog, if they knew it attacked sheep?"

"Denied it. Brazened it out, she did. Naturally, seeing she'd put the dog up to it. He had to put it down when Cutfield said he'd shoot it at sight if he saw it in one of his fields and take Wainwright to court after, with the carcass to prove his case."

"So then the farmer had no more trouble?"

"I didn't say that. There was more attacks on Cutfield's sheep not long before she went."

"Did Mr Cutfield shoot that dog?"

"Never got a sight of it."

"Then it was nothing to do with Mrs Wainwright, was it?"

Winter opened his mouth to explain further, but thought better of it, touched his cap, tucked the parcel of dirty linen under his arm and went down the path to his bicycle, leaning against the hedge outside the gate.

CHAPTER IV

At the end of May, Judy Frost went down to Upfold for a week's holiday. This was early in the year for her, but served two purposes: to see how her parents were getting on in their new home and to give herself a rest after an exceptionally hard-working spring. The severe winter had produced a very large crop of broken ankles and wrists in elderly people from slipping on icy pavements and also many severe burns in homes with faulty heating apparatus. So the occupational therapy department in which Judy worked had been flooded with the aftermath of these calamities.

Judy, who was twenty-eight at this time, came down to Stourfield by train and was met at the station by her mother with the car.

"Your father can't be torn away from the garden," Mrs Frost explained. "He's a perfect maniac over it. I hope he won't give himself a coronary."

When they got back to Upfold they found Dr Frost wrestling with a submerged rose bed. Judy went up to him while her mother disappeared into the house to prepare lunch. Dr Frost greeted his daughter with affection, but did not stop what he was doing. Seeing him so occupied Judy went indoors.

"I see what you mean," she said. "He has a dedicated look in his eye. He'll certainly kill himself if he goes on like this."

"I've persuaded him to order a firm in to do the lawn," Mrs Frost answered. "Take it all up and lay it again with fresh turf. Very expensive but well worth it."

"But all this digging—!"

"He likes digging. He's made a wonderful difference to the garden already. It's really quite well stocked, considering.

I can't think how the plants have survived, all choked by weeds. But a lot of them have."

Judy wandered out again. There was plenty of time, only half the morning gone. She felt the blessed relief and comfort of her temporary release from the clock. She brought in her suitcase from the car, found her bedroom, explored the rest of the house, laid the dining-room table for lunch and went out again to join her father, who was still patiently digging.

"Come and see my new toolshed," he said, striking his fork into the ground and pulling out his handkerchief to wipe his face. "Great improvement. The old hen-house was falling to bits. We've cleared all that away and the wire with it."

"Are you going to join the hen-run up with the lawn or with the kitchen garden?"

Judy was looking at the lush grass that covered the space beside the new shed.

"No. Neither. I want to have a rockery there."

"You mustn't give yourself too much to keep up," she said, slipping her hand under his arm.

He put the arm round her shoulders.

"I won't. But I've nothing else much to do now."

There was no regret in his voice, but he was gazing away into the distance and Judy wondered, not for the first time, whether he had been right to give up his practice so comparatively early.

"What are the people like here?" she asked, following her thought.

"Quite pleasant," he answered. "All very friendly. The vicar's a bit of a nonentity, the doctor's a good chap, I think. Well-liked. You get the impression the older inhabitants still exist in a place and community they've known all their lives, but the young ones use it as a dormitory suburb for Stourfield. Hardly any of them work here. There aren't the jobs."

Judy nodded. This was not quite what she wanted to know.

She thought she would be more likely to get it from her mother.

At lunch Mrs Frost reminded her husband of the cocktail party they were booked to attend that evening.

"You too," she told Judy. "A Mrs Graveney. She had us to tea early on and we've had her back and now, I suppose, this is the next move."

"Are we really going to cultivate Mrs Graveney?" Dr Frost asked, in a rebellious voice.

"Well, I think it's the other way round, isn't it?" his wife said, mildly. "We do want to meet people. We obviously aren't really Mrs Graveney's sort, which must be quite clear to her already. But she wants to be the one to introduce us to Upfold. I don't see any harm in that."

"What's the matter with her?" Judy asked.

"Nothing really," Mrs Frost said.

"Money," Dr Frost growled. "Too much of it. I've seen Graveney, but I've not spoken to him yet. Business—climber—she's pretentious. Can't help it, I suppose."

"I'm all for money," said Judy, laughing.

"What are you doing in the medical profession, then?"

"She entertains quite a lot," Mrs Frost said. "I don't know who goes to her parties. We shall see."

"You think it won't be the right lot?" Judy asked, still laughing. "As if it mattered these days."

They left it at that. Judy helped her mother to clear away the meal and then took the newspaper into a corner of the garden where a small uneven patch of grass had been cleared. Her parents rested indoors.

As Mrs Graveney's house was so near Mulberry Cottage the Frosts walked there that evening. They found a row of cars in the lane, the front door open and the sound of many voices came through it.

"*Big* party," murmured Judy.

It was indeed, and as the Frost parents had expected, the guests were on the whole quite clearly business friends of Mr

Graveney. Their wives were there, expensively dressed, herding together, exchanging familiar jokes with Mrs Graveney whenever she was near them and turning away, with all too obvious boredom, from any local inhabitants to whom they were introduced.

But there were several local people there, notably Dr Marshall and his wife, to whom the Frosts made their way after they had greeted their hostess and been introduced to their host. Mrs Marshall, on greeting Judy, at once exclaimed, "Down for a whole week? You must meet Susan Singleton. I saw her a minute ago with that friend of hers. The dark girl. Now where—?"

"With Julian, if he's arrived, I should think," Dr Marshall said. "Mrs Graveney would never feel her party was complete without him."

"That's Mr Farnham, the author," Mrs Frost explained to Judy. "I've heard of him from several people."

"Our local celebrity," Mrs Marshall said.

Judy had never heard of him.

"What does he write?" she asked. The party had reached the shouting stage, but as so often happens, a momentary lull came just as she spoke, so that her clear voice rang out across the room, making the heads turn in her direction.

"Novels," a voice shouted back from the nearest corner. "Bloody awful, popular novels!"

Judy whipped round, her cheeks flaming. She saw a tall, angular figure pushing towards her. His face, lined, haggard, permanently sun-burned, was at this moment lit by amusement that shone out of his dark eyes, fixed on her as he moved.

"A bit high already," murmured Dr Marshall, then raising his voice said, "Julian, come and meet the Frosts."

"Can't you see that's what I'm trying to do," the newcomer answered, still gazing with arrogant, amused eyes at Judy.

"Dr and Mrs Frost and—Miss Frost."

"Judy," said Judy.

"I've enjoyed your books for years, Mr Farnham," said Mrs

45

Frost at once, anxious to cover up her daughter's unfortunate clanger.

"And you have never heard of me?" he said to Judy, with a very small bow of acknowledgment to her mother.

"No. I'm sorry. I haven't."

"No cause for sorrow. Rather for rejoicing. You've missed nothing, I assure you."

Judy rose to the challenge.

"Mummy should have told me you lived here. Then I would have done my homework."

He laughed. His face showed real amusement.

"This your first visit to Upfold?"

"Yes. The parents only moved into Mulberry Cottage at the beginning of May."

She saw the light fade from his eyes as she said this. The hand that held his glass shook, but nothing was spilled as the glass was nearly empty. With an effort he said, "I'm so bad at listening to names when I'm introduced. What did you say yours was?"

"Frost. Judy Frost."

"Your father is a retired doctor?"

"Yes."

"From London?"

"Yes."

He nodded.

"Of course. I knew, really." He was silent for a few seconds. It seemed to Judy that he had drawn her into a place apart among all this crowd of strangers and that she was quite content to be there, shut off from them, listening to him.

"It's been empty so long."

He meant the cottage, of course, but somehow there was a greater emptiness implied, a huge gap in time or in experience or even in himself.

Astonished at these strange thoughts, Judy could only say, "Yes," waiting for him to go on. She had heard nothing yet of the Wainwrights or of the circumstances of their leaving.

46

But Julian shrugged his shoulders, made a wry face, said, "Your glass is empty," and put out a hand to take it from her. At the same moment one of the hired waitresses came up to supply the need. Both Judy and the writer took filled glasses.

Julian said, "I can see a couple of girls I know signalling from that corner. Come and be introduced."

With a brief look round Judy saw that her parents had moved on, led away by Dr Marshall to meet two men who had just come in with their wives. So she followed Julian and presently found herself talking to Susan Singleton and Olivia Fells-Hartley and a couple of young men whose names were lost to her in the welter of introduction.

The conversation was loud and pointless and repetitive for several minutes. Then Susan drew Judy a little way out of the group.

"I think you are one of the new people at Mulberry Cottage," she said.

"Yes." Judy was getting a little tired of this theme.

"Do you live there or are you visiting?"

"My parents live there. I'm down for a week. I work in London."

"So do I. In a shop that calls itself a boutique. Need I say more?"

Judy laughed.

"I'm an occupational therapist."

"Are you really? A strong-arm girl?"

"No. That's a physio."

"Should I know the difference?"

"Not necessarily. If you haven't any medical connections."

Susan smiled and shook her head.

"Do you play tennis?" she asked.

"Rather badly and I didn't bring my racket down. I'm only here for a week. I thought I'd just be seeing how the parents are making out. Daddy particularly. He's fallen for gardening in a big way. I must say they both look very fit."

"I'll lend you a racket," said Susan, who was not interested in the older Frosts but wanted to secure as many recruits for the tennis court as possible. "Come up and play tomorrow. You must."

"Don't be bullied, Miss Frost," said Julian behind her back. "If you don't want to play the childish game, say so."

"But I do," said Judy. "I like tennis but I'm not much good at it. I don't get enough practice."

"You're a worker?"

"She's an occupational therapist," said Susan. "That's right, isn't it, Judy?"

"Yes. D'you know what that is?" she asked Julian.

"I do, as it happens. So you're a worker?"

"Yes. You are, too, aren't you?"

Again he seemed to have isolated her from the other people in the room. But this time he was not allowed to develop the situation. The other girl, Olivia, appeared beside him and with a direct demand that he could not easily refuse, took him away. He gave Judy a curiously helpless, apologising look as he went. She, left alone, feeling herself no longer wanted in that small circle of friends, wandered slowly through the crowd until she found her parents, who were looking for her in their turn, anxious now to go home.

Judy had a telephone call from Susan directly after breakfast the next morning. The latter had not been able to secure enough people for tennis but would Judy please come to tea and meet the parents? Mrs Frost encouraged her to accept this invitation. Judy did so.

Upfold Hall had been in the Singleton family for about two hundred years. It was a pleasant eighteenth-century house of moderate size built upon the foundations of an earlier building that had been burned down. The baronetcy dated from early Georgian times. Most of the Singletons had been soldiers and it spoke well for the number of male progeny and their powers of survival that the present owner was in direct descent. The heir, Judy learned, had prudently gone into business in order to be able to enjoy his heritage when it passed to him, leaving the army tradition to be upheld by a younger brother. Susan was the only girl and like Judy the youngest of the family.

The latter arrived at the appropriate time and found the older Singletons as pleasant, friendly and unassuming as Susan had shown herself to be the day before. They were interested in her work as an occupational therapist. Sir Felix told her one or two very corny medical anecdotes which he deceivingly connected with his own friends in the usual manner of raconteurs. Lady Singleton asked one or two discreet questions about Dr Frost's career and Mrs Frost's favourite occupations.

"Up to now—since the War, I mean, she's been general dog's body to Daddy and the rest of us," Judy said. "There were no proper servants after the war. Only dailies. I believe we had a nanny when I was very young. I don't really remember her."

"Your mother sounds a very wonderful person," said Lady Singleton. "I hope I shall meet her soon."

"And don't you dare force her into your good works," said Susan. "Or not till she's had a good rest."

"I don't think Mummy really likes resting," said Judy, who knew that her mother needed sympathetic friends with whom to occupy herself in a strenuous fashion, rather than a continuing relaxation in solitude.

After tea the girls went for a walk round the garden, looked at the stables, now occupied by only two surviving hacks, a family car and a jeep, and walked on into the surrounding parkland, where Sir Felix's beef cattle lay in the shade of trees chewing the cud peacefully.

"The stables are a bit of a shambles now," Susan said. "In the old days there was always a string of hunters, but Daddy can't hunt now on account of his leg and the boys have never been keen on riding even, far less on hunting."

"It's usually the girls now, isn't it?" said Judy, who had once had a great desire to manage a horse, but in London had found the whole business too complicated, artificial and expensive.

They left the small park by a gate that led into a narrow lane between high hedges. Walking along this they came out on the bank of the stream that passed Upfold village in a wide curve on its way to join a larger river.

"Oh!" exclaimed Judy, delightedly. "I didn't know we had a real river so near."

Susan was amused.

"You can't do much with it except look at it," she said. "There's no boating, because it has very shallow patches at frequent intervals. The fishing is very carefully preserved. Bathing is dangerous—deep holes and weeds. At least—well, no one cares to bathe in it. It has a very sinister aura for the village."

"What on earth d'you mean?"

"The butcher's little boy was drowned in it."

"How dreadful! But someone always gets drowned in rivers, don't they? I mean children that aren't looked after— allowed to go off and play on their own before they can swim or look after themselves—"

"This was different," Susan said.

Something in her face made Judy shrink from hearing the story but her curiosity got the better of her.

"Tell me."

"You're bound to hear it in time," Susan began, almost apologetically. "It's mixed up with this extraordinary *thing* about Mrs Wainwright."

"Oh, *that*!"

Judy had heard the night before from her parents of the mystery of Celia Wainwright's disappearance from Upfold, of her alleged power over men and animals, of the daily's son who had committed suicide.

"You've heard some things?" Susan asked.

"Yes." Judy told her.

"Exactly. You see the village—or at least the older people in the village—think she was a witch."

50

"Seriously?"

"Quite seriously. I don't know how it began. There's always been an ordinary, sensible explanation of the things that happened, but *someone* must have started the idea and it caught on. So when the little Pawley boy—he was about six, I believe, I don't remember—I was away at school, my third term—when he fell in and she was found kneeling on the bank with a long stick in her hand—obviously trying to help him—they said she'd made him fall in and had pushed him under with the stick."

"How horrible! How *wicked*!"

Judy was revolted, more by the idea that people could believe this possible than by the event, which could be explained quite differently, as Susan had pointed out.

"I suppose Mrs Wainwright couldn't swim?" she asked.

"That's what she said at the inquest, I think. She said the child slipped and fell in, she tried to make him clutch the stick so that she could pull him to the bank, while his little friends ran for help. She was still trying when the help came."

"Too late."

"Yes. The child had drowned."

"But those other children. The ones who ran for help. They knew she had done nothing—only tried to help."

"It was one of them who said at the inquest that she had done it all deliberately."

"Good God!"

Judy was profoundly shocked. That a superstitious rumour of this nature could take such a hold on an entire modern village population was scarcely credible. Only ten years ago. Some old woman had probably started it. A half-crazy old woman. The kind they burned as a witch a couple of hundred years ago. But in 1953—

As if in answer to her thought Susan went on, "There *was* a witch in Upfold in the late eighteenth century. Some time after my family came here. We've got an old diary of the Singleton at that time. He heard a lot of shouting when he was

51

riding in the park and went to see what was happening. They had just thrown this woman into the river to test if she was a witch. She kept coming up and then sinking so they couldn't make up their minds about her."

"What happened?"

"My great-great-great-grandfather or whatever he was rode his horse into the water and scooped the poor thing out and took her up to the house and revived her."

"What happened then?"

"The diary doesn't say. Maddening things, diaries, aren't they? Always miss the really plummy bits."

They turned back from the river which had now lost its charm for Judy, and re-entered the park.

"So there is a kind of tradition of witchcraft in Upfold?" Judy said after a long, thoughtful pause.

"I suppose the old story would make it easier for them to swallow the new one."

"That's what I meant. But there must have been something about her, too. Something queer, sinister, evil, perhaps."

"I wouldn't know. Daddy and Mummy never talk about her at all. They just won't."

"But the other people who live here? Mr Shalford wouldn't be much good against the devil, Mummy says—"

"Too true!"

"But there must be someone who sees it all sensibly. What about Mr Farnham? He was here then, wasn't he? He'd be quite young then and not superstitious, surely?"

Susan gave a short laugh.

"Julian is just about the last person you can ask," she said. "He's supposed to have been having an affair with the witch and he certainly left Upfold the night she disappeared and didn't come back for three weeks."

"*Really?*"

"Oh yes. Olivia—you know—the girl who was here yesterday—she's a friend of his and he actually told her this. But

52

he didn't tell her if they went off together or how it broke up in the end. He never tells anyone that."

"I suppose he likes to be mysterious because he's a romantic novelist," said Judy, with contempt. She was annoyed with herself now for certain uncontrolled, romantic thoughts she had allowed herself on the evening before when she got back from the party.

The afternoon with the Singletons was followed by three days of blissful emptiness for Judy. She helped her mother in the house and her father in the garden. She explored the village and the surrounding countryside. She bowed to Mrs Graveney and other new acquaintances when she met them in the shops or the village street. She introduced her mother to Lady Singleton at the Post Office counter of the general store. The Frosts drove to the coast at Wittering one afternoon and all of them bathed in a very chilly sea. Apart from these mild activities Judy did nothing and made no new friends. Susan Singleton had gone back to London on Sunday night to start work on Monday in her boutique.

On Friday Judy realised with something of a shock that she had only two more whole days of her holiday left. She was on her way back to Mulberry Cottage with some shopping when a car drew up beside her and Julian Farnham leaned out.

"Can I give you a lift anywhere?" he asked.

Judy laughed.

"I'm only twenty yards from home," she said.

"I know."

The queer look she had seen before was on his face again and added to it a kind of helplessness that she suddenly found appealing.

"Thank you all the same," she said, smiling and beginning to walk on.

He drove the car slowly beside her until they reached the gate.

"Shove those things inside," he said, "and come for a drive with me."

It was what she had really wanted all the week, she knew. But it was only half an hour to lunch time; the parents expected her to be in.

"Tell them you're going out to lunch," Julian said.

"Am I?"

"Yes."

Five minutes later they were threading a tortuous but beautiful back way, far from main roads, towards the South Downs. They had lunch at a village inn, climbed the hill behind it, stood on springy turf with the downs rolling away before them and the sea sparkling beyond. They did not talk much; they were profoundly happy. Only when they were in the car again, speeding back along the main road now in the direction of Upfold, Julian said, with a kind of angry sorrow, "Why didn't I meet you before?"

"Before what?" Judy asked, very gently.

"So they've been gossipping about me?" His answer was immediate and bitter.

"Who d'you mean?"

"Susan—Olivia—the Graveney woman—"

"No one has gossipped," said Judy firmly. "I wouldn't listen—no, that's not true—of course I'd listen, but I wouldn't pay much attention—"

"Wouldn't you?" His voice went soft. "No, I don't think you would."

Encouraged by this Judy said bravely, "But Susan did say something about Mrs Wainwright—the horrible things the village thought about her. Witchcraft and all that nonsense—"

"Stop!" he cried out. He brought the car on to the verge of the road, switched off the engine and turned towards her.

"When I went to live at Upfold," he said, slowly, "I'd just been given a literary prize for my first novel. I'd saved a bit of money while I was in the Army doing National Service, and in a job I got just after it. With the prize I thought I could make out for two years and write another book, perhaps two, and establish myself."

54

"Well?"

He had stopped speaking. He was staring ahead of him now, all the haggard lines of his face rousing her indignant pity.

"She wrecked all that. Oh, I'm established all right. I'm rich. I'm well known—now. In ten years or so I'll have faded so completely I might never have existed."

"You mean because you write popular romance? Why do you, then? If you'd really wanted to write seriously you would have, wouldn't you? In spite of anything—or anyone? I mean you'd rather have killed her than your own integrity—wouldn't you? No one could make you betray your talent if it was a true one."

His face went very white.

"It was a true one and I ruined it," he said. "She was capable of anything—*anything*!"

CHAPTER V

Judy saw Julian again on Saturday and briefly on Sunday. The Frosts asked him to lunch on the latter date, but he made a trivial excuse. To avoid going into Mulberry Cottage, Judy thought.

He did not speak again about Celia Wainwright and the girl had enough good sense and right feeling to curb her curiosity, which had plagued her increasingly since his outburst on Friday. But though they did not approach this particular intimacy, in other ways their friendship's quick flowering went on unhindered. Judy went back to London with a promise to meet him there soon for an evening at the ballet and a firm determination in her own mind to spend as many weekends as possible at her home.

On Sunday evening the fine dry weather broke and it rained steadily all night. On Monday morning Dr Frost took advantage of the softened soil to attack the surface of the old hen-run. The turves came up easily, the earth below was pleasant to work. At about the centre of the run and two spits down Dr Frost began to dig up bones.

At first he thought he had turned up the relics of mutton joints thrown to the hens to supplement their diet. He threw the fragments aside. But the yield continued. A succession of whole ribs was followed by some long bones that clearly had nothing to do with any joint for the table or for that matter with any domestic quadruped. He recognised that what he was digging up was a human skeleton.

At this Dr Frost paused and quietly assembled what he had already found. By great good fortune he had not broken any long bone, but he had scattered a number of small ones which on closer inspection he recognised as belonging to a wrist. After that he went to work very carefully and methodically, arranging his astonishing find in several groups, digging and checking and sieving the earth until he completed a limb and another and so on till the thing lay before him, screened from the house and the road by bushes.

At lunch time he covered the whole with sacks and went indoors. He determined not to tell his wife about it just yet. The skeleton was complete or very nearly so and it belonged, he had decided, to a woman. This was easy to know on account of the general shape and measurements of the pelvis, the small-ness and delicacy of the bones and the shallow grooves of the muscular attachments on them. But he had not yet found the skull and he wanted very much to make the whole discovery himself. He did not relish the idea of others digging on his property, with no regard for his plans for the garden nor for the work he had already done in it.

After lunch Mrs Frost took the car into Stourfield. Her husband, she thought, would rest until tea-time, when she would be back to pick him up and take him off to tea with some of their new friends.

As soon as she had gone the doctor went back to his search but though he dug up the whole run and measured and checked the probable position of the head when the body was buried, he found no trace of a skull anywhere. But he did find one suggestive clue to its disappearance. The spine was not complete. The first and second cervical vertebrae were missing and the third showed signs of injury. The head, he concluded, had been removed and by violence. After, or at the time of, death, he wondered, with a shudder. In any case, he could obviously keep the find to himself no longer. He transferred the remains to the carpenter's bench in his new shed, laying them out in an orderly manner to form a recumbent skeleton. A woman, certainly, he thought, between five foot three and five foot six, though this was the roughest of guesses with no indication of the size of the head and in any case it was a very ordinary height for a woman. As he bent over the bones he noticed that the right clavicle had been broken at some time during life and had mended without deformity. A good result, he noted with approval. There was an injury, too, which he did not understand, to the breast bone and cracks in two of the left side ribs that joined this bone. Putting these four specimens, together with the third cervical verebra, on one side, Dr Frost covered up the rest with sacking. Then, folding his specimens in a piece of old newspaper he found in the shed he carried them back to the house and locked them in a drawer of his desk in his own room. After that he went to the telephone to call the village constable, a man named Galton.

Though his main interest hitherto had lain in unearthing the wholly unexpected contents of the hen-run, he had naturally wondered, with growing interest and dread, whose these bones were and how long they had lain concealed. To conclude at once that they must be the bones of Mrs Wainwright, simply because she was said to have disappeared, was a natural reaction but not necessarily the right solution. On the other hand

57

this was the secret burial of some woman or girl who had suffered undoubted violence, perhaps in the manner of her death, perhaps to her dead body after death. In any case a matter, alas, for the police.

The constable was out. A woman's voice explained that he was in Stourfield at the juvenile court.

"Those hooligans that broke in our Club last week, sir," she said. "Frank's giving evidence on the two he caught at it."

"You are Mrs Galton?"

"Yes, sir. I'll tell him to ring you directly he gets back, shall I?"

Dr Frost considered. This might be at any time. The bones had obviously waited many years for discovery. They could wait a bit longer. He would keep his tea date. Besides, he did not want to raise an alarm prematurely.

"Tell him I'm going to be out for tea but home about six."

"Then it's not urgent, sir?"

Her persistence annoyed Dr Frost. He thought he had made this quite clear. So he forgot his usual complete reticence. Perhaps he was out of practice in the exercise of that invincible patience he had learned over the years of his professional life. Perhaps it was partly due to an excitement he had felt more deeply than he acknowledged.

"It is and it isn't," he said, irritably. "As a matter of fact it's something I've found buried in my hen-run. Been there a long time, tell him. I want his advice. It's—well—it's a thing it's my duty to report."

"Yes?"

The voice was eager, carefully controlled, but very eager. Dr Frost was warned.

"That's all. Tell him to come straight to my garden shed at six o'clock. I'll be there waiting for him."

"Very good, sir."

The time was then three-fifteen, the doctor noted. He settled himself to read the newspaper, but found he could not concentrate. He got out his specimens from the drawer, looked

58

at them again very carefully, made no progress and put them away as before.

He sighed, staring out of the window, seeing all too clearly the end of his present peaceful existence, his new garden ruined or rather its making postponed, the rumours, the speculations, the newspaper publicity. Why had he not quietly re-buried his nasty find and said nothing about it? That was what Upfold would want to know. The gentry because they hated all forms of publicity; the village—because they had hated Mrs Wainwright? *Was* it then Mrs Wainwright? If not, what further dark history would Upfold disclose? What other disappearance had there been, of several years standing, of a woman, certainly?

In any case who had made this illegal concealment of death, to put the criminal aspect at its lowest? For what purpose? Naturally to conceal a greater crime. The absence of a skull pointed all too clearly at murder. But they would search for the skull. All over the garden, all over the house, too, perhaps?

Dr Frost groaned aloud. He had behaved correctly, responsibly and must now suffer the consequences. Turning once more to the newspaper he decided, between paragraphs barely understood, not to tell his wife anything until after the constable had seen the remains.

So the tea-party was a success, unmarred for Mrs Frost and in some measure a solace for the doctor. Their hosts were also a retired pair, living at the foot of the downs on the other side of Stourfield, the husband an old Cambridge undergraduate contemporary of Henry Frost, he discovered. They had not known each other when they were up. They were both amused and Dr Frost found it a relief to talk of former times and to be free from any need to discuss his reasons for choosing Upfold as his place of retirement. This customary subject for question and answer did not occur to his host, who had made his own choice for family reasons and assumed that the Frosts had done likewise. Nor was Dr Frost asked about his tastes, his hobbies or his professional past. The last few weeks in

Upfold, he realised, had been a bit of a bore in this respect.

Meanwhile Mrs Frost had learned the connection between her hostess and the Singletons and why she and her husband had been at the Graveney's party ten days ago.

"With an ulterior motive," she was told. "Subscription hunting in an underhand and indirect manner. We were dragged in by Dr Marshall's partner and now I can ask Mrs Graveney back and work on her."

"Disgraceful," said her husband, "but I've no doubt you'll pull it off."

"And they say the British have no understanding of politics," said Mrs Frost, laughing. "How wrong can you be?"

The Frosts stayed longer with their new friends than they intended and so did not arrive home until well after six. As he drove into his garage Dr Frost saw a bicycle propped up against the side of it and near the front door the constable, in uniform, holding his helmet in his hand and mopping his forehead with a dark blue handkerchief.

"Sorry to keep you waiting, officer," Dr Frost said, hurrying up to him and leaving his wife to fasten the garage doors. "Nattering with friends who have also recently come to these parts."

"A lot of gentlemen do settle hereabouts," said Galton, mildly. "I went to the garden shed, sir, as directed, but seeing the garage empty and not getting an answer at any of the doors I concluded you was delayed."

"Come along then," Dr Frost said, leading the way down the garden and feeling in his pocket for the key of the shed as he went.

It was dark inside, after the bright glow of the sunset sky over the garden. But even so, as he removed the sacks, Dr Frost was aware of a change in the specimens he had laid there a few hours before. He fumbled again in his jacket pocket. No spectacle case. Of course, he had changed for the tea-party. It was in his old working jacket.

"I must get my glasses," he said. "But this is what I found

when I dug my hen-run today. A human skeleton, as you see. I won't be a minute."

Ignoring the constable's startled exclamation, he hurried indoors. His wife met him in the hall.

"What's that policeman doing here?" she asked. "You were expecting him. Why?"

"My glasses," he said. "Forgot to take them with me. Now, where—?"

"Bother your glasses. You haven't answered my question."

She had followed him to his desk where he had gone first. He often hung his gardening jacket over the back of it, but it was not there.

"Upstairs, I suppose." He was already retreating, colliding with her in the doorway. "I'll tell you later, Jeanie. Didn't want to spoil the afternoon."

"Spoil—?"

It was no use. He had gone and she knew better than to follow him to his bedroom. In a few seconds he was clattering down again, out at the front door and down the garden to the shed. She laughed gently, being used to her man and confident she would hear all in due course.

When Dr Frost re-entered the shed he found Constable Galton standing near the small window staring at a thigh-bone he held in his hand. Without speaking he handed it to the doctor and waited.

Dr Frost saw, when he had put on his spectacles, that the bone he held was not one of those he had dug up in the garden. It was longer, thicker, and definitely male. Moreover it had areas marked upon it in different coloured paints. The earth that smeared it in part rubbed away easily, leaving a polished surface beneath.

Meeting the constable's impassive gaze he moved back to the table. Together they inspected the rest of the find. Dr Frost saw that the general arrangement of the skeleton lying there was unaltered. It was all set out as he had put his roughly together. But now the two halves by no means matched one another. The long bones of one side were shorter than those of the other. The rib cage had belonged to a smallish individual; the pelvis, a masculine one, to a large person.

Dr Frost picked up several individual bones and stared at them. The constable did likewise. At last the doctor said, controlling his voice with difficulty, "These are anatomical specimens, as I think you have noticed."

"It crossed my mind, sir," Galton said, respectfully. Then he smiled. "If I may say so, it looks to me like a hoax."

So that was how it was to be played, Dr Frost thought, his mind racing. Was this man in it, too? His wife must have picked up the meaning of his own guarded reference to a find. This was the answer. Upfold was more formidable than he had imagined.

It occurred to him that he might have rung up the County police instead of the local man, or even the police station in Stourfield. Comparatively few village constables remained these days, he knew. It had pleased him to think they had one at hand. Now he was not so pleased.

He was still looking at Constable Galton, trying to discover, behind that stolid countenance, how much the man knew or guessed, how much he understood the implications of this duel.

"A hoax." He repeated Galton's words, thoughtfully, quietly.

"Our young lads are always up to mischief," the constable said. "Nothing vicious, mind you. Not like that Stourfield gang I was on to this morning at the court. Borstal for two of them, D.C. the rest."

"You'd better take this away and return it to the owners, if you can find them," Dr Frost said, coldly. "I don't imagine those owners had any part in this nonsense. I certainly hope not. So they may want to take action of some sort, for theft, perhaps. Personally, I don't propose to make any sort of charge."

"No, sir."

"I'll get you some newspaper," the doctor said. "Or will this do?"

He pulled out a couple of large brown paper bags left by the builders when they put up the shed.

"I'll manage," Galton said. He was completely mystified by the whole thing. What an idea, to serve the old boy like this! Giving him a fright first, as they meant to. He hadn't properly looked, of course, or he'd never have been deceived. Even he himself could see the difference.

"I'll find the lads that put up this lark," he said, taking the wrapped bundle under his arm and moving towards the door of the shed.

"I hope you do."

Dr Frost's tone was so different that the constable stopped to look back at him.

"I hope you do," the latter said again and went on, furiously, "Did they think I was too doddering to know the difference?"

Galton made a soothing rejoinder and rode off on his bicycle with the bundle under his arm. Old people had to be humoured, he reflected. They never recognised their failing powers. He told his wife this when he got home, for he could not help thinking the hoax had its funny side. She agreed with him, though in rather a tight-lipped manner. But that was her usual reluctant way with his little jokes.

Dr Frost went indoors and poured out the whole story to his wife.

"You mean they—whoever *they* are—exchanged these anatomy school bones for the skeleton you found? And thought you'd not notice the difference?"

"Apparently."

"Thinking you'd treat it as a hoax and that would be that?"

"Unfortunately for them they've made me keener than ever to find out the truth. Now I know there's someone in Upfold, more than one, I suspect, who has something to hide."

"But what can you do? They've got all the real bones now, haven't they?"

"Not all of them. No."

Dr Frost took her to the drawer in his desk and laid before her the mended clavicle, the injured sternum and ribs and the split third cervical vertebra.

CHAPTER VI

The next morning saw Dr Frost back in the garden, still digging in the old chicken run. He had no hope of finding the skull belonging to the skeleton, but he wanted to make sure it was not there. Also he was determined to complete the set of bones. A few of the small wrist and ankle bones had been missing from his own collection the previous day, though present among the specimens exchanged for his find. Which proved quite conclusively both the ignorance of those who had made the exchange and the haste with which they had done it.

As he expected he did not find the skull, either entire or in fragments, but he found, just below the level of his former digging, a rounded piece of wood, about eighteen inches long and an inch in girth, sharpened at one end. The surface was rough and partly splintered and it was dark with age and long exposure to damp earth.

Dr Frost held it for some minutes, considering. This, too, might be of significance, of very grim significance. He took it, together with his spade, back to the shed, and fetching a rake, smoothed over the surface where he had dug so thoroughly. Then, returning the rake, too, to the shed and taking his new find with him, he went back to the house.

That afternoon Dr Frost drove to London and put his car in the row of marked parking places reserved for the staff near the entrance doors of St Edmund's Hospital. He felt that he was entitled to do so, partly by reason of his long association with the place, partly because his mission was sufficiently serious to warrant such behaviour.

Nodding to the hall porter who was too young to know him but recognised the signs of familiarity and the general appearance of the old man, Dr Frost made his way to the new pathology department and to that part of it where Dr Philip Wallace had his office. When he himself had been resident houseman, Dr Wallace was a first year student. He was now senior morbid anatomist in the Medical School and a forensic pathologist frequently consulted in criminal cases in London and the Home Counties.

Dr Frost was relieved to find the pathologist in his office. He had considered telephoning in advance but rightly feared his way would be blocked by secretarial zealous care or officiousness. As it was he overbore one young woman's objections by asserting both his age and his long-standing acquaintance with Dr Wallace. He was relieved and amused when the latter greeted him with warmth and recognition. The young woman retreated, looking sulky.

"You're protected by very adequate dragons, Philip," he said, after shaking hands.

"In their own interests, most probably," Wallace answered. "They're afraid I'll stay on chatting when they want to get away. It happens too often, I fear."

"It might happen today," said Dr Frost.

He unwrapped the parcel he was carrying and explained exactly what he had found the day before and that morning.

Dr Wallace's interest was immediately engaged. He gave each specimen a rapid but detailed examination and then leaned back, looking with bright eyes at his elderly colleague.

"You're perfectly right it's a woman," he said." At a first inspection I'd say a young one, not over twenty-five. This clavicle is just about ossified, I should say. Not long since the process was completed. Been buried up to ten years, probably. I'm only guessing. Have to make tests on all that, of course."

"Ten years ago," said Dr Frost, "a young woman married

to the former owner of my new house, disappeared one night and has not been seen or heard of in Upfold since."

"Sounds like a Victorian melodrama," said Wallace, who was turning the ribs over and over in his hands. "D'you mean to say they never heard where she'd gone? Married, did you say? Surely her husband found her?"

"I don't think so. I'm not sure. I haven't made any inquiries in that direction. But there is a very definite air of scandal. I've heard hints from time to time that she ran off with an Upfold man. Having an affair, I suppose."

"That sounds more likely."

"But if this *is* Mrs Wainwright, she never left the village at all."

"Husband did her in? Buried her in the hen run? Has a familiar air. Jealous?"

"He was away in London that night and the next night. When he came back and found her gone he went back to London himself and never saw Upfold again. Or so the story runs."

Dr Wallace shook his head.

"All very vague," he said. "But you'll have to report it to the police. Concealing a death is a criminal offence."

"I have reported it to the police—local chap. We still have a village constable, believe it or not. This is the oddest part of the whole thing."

After he had heard of the so-called hoax Dr Wallace agreed.

"Somebody knows who the skeleton was and wants to keep it hidden still," he said.

"Obviously. Moreover they've got it all now, except these bits here."

"You're right." Dr Wallace's voice was even more emphatic than before. This was the sort of challenge he delighted in and which had brought him to his present eminence. He stared at the fragments on the desk, listening carefully as Dr Frost went on.

"Of course they'll destroy it all now. They think they've got the lot. I said nothing to Galton. Let him think I was fooled. They must have taken the head at the start. Chopped it off, don't you think?"

"Probably." Dr Wallace took a lens to the vertebra, then laid it down and took up again separately the ribs and sternum. "Did you do this, digging them up?" he asked Frost.

"I did not. I went very carefully after I found the first ulna. But I have an idea what did cause the damage." Dr Frost pushed forward the piece of wood.

"This stake," he said. "I found it this morning. You may think I'm being fantastic. I did until today. But there is a definite belief in the village that Mrs Wainwright was a witch."

"Good God!"

Dr Wallace snatched up the piece of wood and studied it intently. When he put it down again, which he did very carefully, he said, "Fantastic, as you say. But if it's true, that someone or some people cut off this woman's head and buried her with a stake driven through her heart, then we're back in the middle ages and my guess is the village killed her and the village knows who actually did it and who disposed of the body. The husband was away, you said?"

"Away on business—middle of each week. Everyone knew this was how he lived. Long weekends at Upfold, Tuesday and Wednesday, sometimes Thursday, too, in town. Must have had a flat or rooms of some kind in London."

Dr Wallace nodded.

"Too easy. But I can't understand why he never made a fuss when she disappeared. I mean a private inquiry would soon settle if she'd run off with someone. A quiet divorce—or even no divorce, a simple separation. The village might not get to know about that, though I doubt it. But I'd have thought her own friends—"

"They are totally reticent," said Dr Frost. "Those I have met in Upfold, I mean. They hint, they guess, but I'm pretty sure they know nothing."

67

"How long had she been married to this man?"

"According to what I've been told about two years. He was in Upfold before and brought her there directly after the marriage, I understand."

"Then she must have had friends of her own elsewhere. Where did she come from?"

"Nobody knows."

"Never had any friends of her own down to the cottage?"

"Look," said Dr Frost, beginning to become exasperated by so many questions he could not answer. "I haven't begun to find these things out for myself. I came to you to get light on these very few remains. I'm not the right person to conduct a full investigation."

The two men fell silent for a few seconds. Then Dr Wallace pressed a button on his desk and a secretary appeared. He asked her to get one of his laboratory assistants to come down to the office.

"Jenkins, if he's up there," he said. "But someone—at once."

"Yes, sir."

"I'll have this stick examined for blood and so on," Dr Wallace explained, when the girl had gone. "Even now it may show something. This very dark stain here." He pointed it out. "Then we'll establish the age of the bones and the length of time they've been in the ground. Will you send me samples of the earth, too, please? At the depth you dug up the bones."

"I'll try. I've filled in the hole, as a matter of fact."

"Pity. But never mind. Do the best you can."

"Certainly. Anything else?"

"You can find out where those anatomy school bones came from. Or can't you?"

"Galton—the local cop—took them away."

"Then he'll have given them back, if he knows. *Is* he in this?"

"I don't think so. But I'll find out. Actually I have an idea for one set."

"Oh yes?"

"The brother of one of our local farmers, man called Cutfield, is in medicine."

"Not *our* Jim Cutfield?"

"He qualified from here, yes. I've been meaning to look him up. He was in Upfold on holiday recently."

Dr Wallace rose to his feet.

"If it's the same Cutfield he's taking his Primary in a few weeks' time."

"Anatomy!"

"Exactly. You'll probably find him over in the Medical School at this moment. Ask him if he took his bones home to revise and left them there. Or better still, get your local bobby to call at the farmer's place and inquire."

"I think I'll try to contact young Cutfield now before I go back," Dr Frost said. "I think we ought to go on playing the hoax at present. Don't want Upfold to know what we're doing or we'll never get anywhere."

"Sooner or later I'll have to report this," Dr Wallace said as he opened the door of his room for the visitor. "You realise that, don't you, Harry? But I'll keep you posted. And I hope you'll do the same for me."

As Dr Frost turned away he met a tall young man with a long white coat, unbuttoned, flapping round him, striding forward towards the room he was leaving.

"Oh, there you are, Jenkins," he heard Dr Wallace say. "I've a job for you I want done at once."

Reminding himself to get a specimen of earth sent off to the pathologist the next day, Dr Frost set about finding young Cutfield and ran him down in the refectory of the Medical School where he was drinking a large cup of coffee in an attempt to stimulate his flagging brain, exhausted by intensive revision of his examination subjects. Dr Frost's unexpected appearance and still more his astonishing story were just what he needed.

To begin with the two men exchanged the usual expressions of surprise at the small size of the world they lived in, after which Dr Frost said, "I've been meaning to look you up since I heard from your brother that you were at St Edmund's. But now I've a special reason for it—rather a serious one, in a way."

And he told young Cutfield of his discovery of the bones, not mentioning the fact of the substitution.

"A thoroughly silly try-on," he finished. "Even Galton recognised them for what they are. The point is, could one half skeleton have been yours? Did anyone at Upfold borrow your set for any reason?"

"No. They didn't. But I left the bones down there by mistake the last time I was at the farm. I'm going down next week-end, actually."

"Then you'll be able to identify them?"

"Certainly I will. If they are mine. I hope they're all right?"

"They had earth over them, of course," said the doctor, truthfully and went no further. Instead, he asked quietly, "Did your brother know you had the bones with you?"

"Everyone there knew," Cutfield answered. "It was a sort of silly joke round the farm. You know the way people go on about bones and dissection—"

"Yes."

So anyone on the farm could have taken the bones, provided they had access to where they were kept. At this stage, not wanting to appear too eager for information Dr Frost decided he would not ask any more questions. He spent another quarter of an hour in general conversation, invited Cutfield to ring him up at Mulberry Cottage when next he visited Upfold and left the young man to get on with his tedious preparation for the forth-coming Primary examination, the necessary first step towards the surgical Fellowship.

On his arrival home Mrs Frost greeted him with a telephone message from Constable Galton. The latter had been to Cutfield's farm. The farmer knew his young brother had left his set of bones there, but when he took Galton to look at them the two men found the cupboard where they had lain empty except for the skull that formed part of the set.

"The skull," said Dr Frost aloud, thoughtfully. He looked up at his wife.

"You took this message?"

"I did."

"You notice the skull was left behind when someone brought the rest of Cutfield's set here?"

"There was no skull in the shed, was there?"

"There was no skull in the ground. It looks as if our hoaxer knew this, too."

Mrs Frost nodded.

"It would be a difficult point for them. If they knew you wouldn't find a skull because no skull was ever buried, then you certainly wouldn't believe the specimens were the bones you'd dug up if a skull appeared with them."

"Tricky for the bastards, wasn't it?"

He was becoming angry again at the thought of this feeble attempt to deceive an experienced man.

Mrs Frost said, soothingly, "They must be very worried people, whoever they are, whoever the skeleton belongs to. What did Philip Wallace say?"

Her husband told her.

"Then you'd better have a word with Galton," she said. "Congratulate him on finding out where some of the bones belong. Tell him you've seen Mr Cutfield's brother, so that clinches it. I wonder where they got hold of the other half?"

"In Upfold," said Dr Frost. "Almost certainly. There wasn't much time, you see. It was nearly three when I first rang up Galton. We went out at four and came back around half-past six. They must have known straight away where to get hold of the bones to fix it all so promptly."

"How did they manage to get into the shed?" Mrs Frost asked. "You locked the door, didn't you?"

Dr Frost made a wry face.

"And left the window open," he said. "It's a small window, but a thin type could worm his way in."

"Or a young boy—or girl?"

"Exactly."

Later that day Dr Frost went to see Dr Marshall. He found him in his garden, cutting off dead tulip heads.

"Didn't know you took an interest," Dr Frost told him.

"I'm not a fanatic, like you," Marshall answered. "But I like to do my bit in keeping it tidy. Besides, the waiting room looks out this side. Mustn't let the patients think we're a slovenly lot."

They laughed. Dr Frost saw an opening which could lead to his purpose in being there. So he took it and presently Dr Marshall led him into the house and into the surgery.

"I kept my set," he said. "Unlike most students who sell them on to their successors the first time they get in the red after they qualify."

He opened a cupboard that was not locked and rummaged among some large cardboard boxes at the bottom of it. But with no result. After pulling out the whole of the contents, which included boxes of slides, old instruments, a few out of date text books and a microscope in a wooden case, he straightened up, saying in a bewildered, angry voice, "They've gone! And I know they were here a week ago."

"You're sure of that?"

"Perfectly sure. Look here, Frost, what's all this in aid of?"

Dr Frost told him about the hoax. Marshall sat down at his desk, too surprised at first to think clearly. But it did not take him long to come to all those conclusions Dr Frost had reached already. The latter, watching him, felt assured that he had had no part in arranging the substitution.

"Who would know you had those bones in the cupboard?" he asked.

"Any member of my household. Possibly a few of the patients."

"When you say household, you include staff?"

"Yes, of course. My wife helps in the spring-cleaning, which is why it goes on so long and is so damnably thorough. But Mrs Thompson does the bulk of it."

"Mrs *Thompson?*"

"Yes."

Dr Marshall looked steadily across the table.

"You haven't said it, Frost, but you think the bones you found belong to Mrs Wainwright, don't you?"

"It is possible, isn't it? She is said to have disappeared—"

"She did disappear. That is the simplest way of saying what happened. None of us ever saw her again. She was here one day and on the next she wasn't. No inquiries, no official inquiries, as you know. But a lot of us tried to find out where she was. Impossible. Wainwright himself would say nothing. Not a word. I had a special reason for wanting to see him, but he would not see me. I couldn't get in touch with him anywhere. Always he'd just left or was in conference or some other damned silly excuse. I've always imagined he found her and they settled again somewhere else or they agreed to part."

"Other people besides you tried to find out. What about Julian Farnham?"

"Why d'you say that?" Dr Marshall's face hardened.

"He went away the same night, didn't he?"

"He came back, three weeks later, alone."

"That's all you know?"

"That's all I'm prepared to say. Except that she did break her collar bone. Riding with the Singletons, her first year here."

Dr Frost moved towards the door.

"I understand," he said. "I'm not pressing you. It's not my job, thank God. But I'm going to find out who my skeleton belonged to. Wallace will have to inform the police when he's finished his tests. I'm pretty certain in my own mind that Upfold has something to hide, something hideous, perhaps.

You'll have to be prepared to help eventually, you know, Marshall."

Dr Marshall said nothing until he had seen Dr Frost back to his car. Then, looking away into the distance, he said, "I'll get in touch with Galton. Have a look at the bones. If they're mine I'll take steps to find who had the bloody sauce to drag me—" He turned his gaze to Dr Frost; his eyes were blazing with anger—"into this *again*!" he finished and turned on his heel and strode away.

CHAPTER VII

Judy, in response to a guarded letter from her father, went down to Upfold again the following weekend, arriving in time for supper on Friday evening. Afterwards Dr Frost told his wife and daughter exactly what had happened since his discovery of the bones in the hen-run.

Mrs Frost had heard most of it before, but to Judy the whole thing came as a shock, an almost unbelievable shock. But it cleared her mind on one point.

"Now I understand something Julian said to me," she explained. "He said Celia was capable of anything. I think he meant her going away without a word to him or anyone. But of course, she hadn't gone. Someone had murdered her."

"You're jumping a number of dubious hurdles to reach that conclusion," her father said. "But never mind that for the moment. Who can have done it? Wainwright himself was in London."

Judy smiled scornfully.

"Have they checked his alibi?" she asked. "Can they account for him right through that Wednesday and Thursday, day and night? Couldn't he have driven down in the

74

middle of the night, killed her, buried her and driven back again?"

"Possibly. Except that his car was here. At least, one car was here. Perhaps he had two. Anyway, he always went up and came back by train."

"You know that? You know he went by train this time?"

"If Marshall's speaking the truth."

"Is he in on this?"

"Since he got his bones back from Galton he's very much in on it. But with reservations towards me. He knows more than he's told me. A good deal more than he's let on to Galton."

"Anyway," Judy said, pursuing her theory, "that husband of hers could have hired a car to drive down in, couldn't he?"

And there they left it, the parents unwilling to carry forward a discussion about Julian Farnham's part in the ten year old mystery. They were not very happy about Judy's rapidly developing friendship with the writer. He was not at all the sort of son-in-law they hoped for.

As for Judy, she shrank from any further revelations of Julian's association with Celia. She had no prudish sentiments about his probable past. The Celia affair was over ten years ago, in any case. Ancient history. A very young man's infatuation for—not an older woman—but someone who, more and more, seemed to assume ageless attributes of sensuality and power.

This aspect of Dr Frost's problem was made more positive still by a visitor who came unasked to Mulberry Cottage the following afternoon. She called to make herself known to them, she said, because she was away at the time of Mrs Graveney's party.

Judy, who opened the door to her, saw a woman with greying, longish hair hanging about her face, an untidy flowered cotton dress and a cardigan drooping at the sides. She wore sandals of plain brown leather on her rather large,

75

bare feet and carried a school satchel with a long loaf of French bread sticking out of it.

"I'm Mabel Snell," she said, edging forward as Judy stood aside for her to enter. "I have the cottage with the studio in Farr's Lane. I paint."

She looked inquiringly, but without hope, for signs of recognition. But Judy was as ignorant of modern painters in the second class as she was of similar writers. So she merely smiled, repeated, "Do come in," and added, "Daddy's gardening as usual, but I'll find my mother for you."

Miss Snell allowed herself to be placed in the sitting room where Mrs Frost joined her daughter at once. Very soon the artist came to the real point of her visit.

"I was so intrigued by this hoax," she said. "The bones, I mean. Gruesome idea." She gave a pleasurable shiver. "Young people do think up the most bizzare, grotesque ideas these days, don't they? No wonder some of their drawings— But I mustn't bore you with my kind of shop."

"You don't," said Mrs Frost, sincerely. "After a lifetime in a doctor's house, I'm out of my depth, but I do enjoy other kinds of talk."

"It seemed to me a morbid expression of a real local neurosis," said Miss Snell and paused to let this sink in.

"I don't quite follow," said Mrs Frost, politely.

"I do," said Judy. "You think the village did this hoax, thought of it, I mean, because they have an idea at the back of their minds that Mrs Wainwright, a witch, has never really left Upfold. That's what you meant, isn't it?"

"Did Julian tell you that?" Miss Snell asked, simply.

"*No!*" Judy's face was scarlet; she was suddenly very angry indeed. "How could he? Why should he? I—I hardly know him."

"I'm sorry." Miss Snell's face showed no contrition, rather a sharp amusement. "I'm very sorry, I gathered you were friends. Village gossip, as usual, I suppose."

Mrs Frost intervened.

76

"You spoke as if Mr Farnham were an authority on village thoughts and doings. Did you mean that? I know he's been here a long time and writers have to be observant people, curious about other people, always looking for copy, analysing—"

"Oh, you make him sound a positive monster," said Miss Snell, jerking in her chair. "He isn't like that at all. But it's common knowledge, I mean you must have been told of his—his friendship with Celia Wainwright?"

"Why don't you say straight out it was an affair?" asked Judy, harshly. "You mean that, don't you?"

Miss Snell recovered her dignity.

"I only know he was terribly upset when she went," she said. "He and I were friends from the time he came here, so naturally he came to me in his distress. He was very young. It had been a ghastly shock for him."

She spoke with real affection. Mrs Frost thought, poor woman, she was in love with him. Perhaps she still is. Judy thought, "So what? She was jealous of Celia. That's about all there is to it." Aloud she said, "But he got over it, of course?"

"Yes, he got over it." Miss Snell gave a slightly contemptuous laugh. "He got older. He didn't take life so seriously. Witness the Olivia affair."

"What about Olivia? D'you mean Susan Singleton's friend? A tall dark girl?"

"Olivia Fells-Hartley. Yes. Haven't you heard about her and Julian?"

"We met both girls at Mrs Graveney's," said Mrs Frost, as Judy remained silent and looked stricken. She added coldly, "We haven't your sources of information, I'm afraid, Miss Snell."

"Have I said something wrong? Have I been indiscreet?"

Miss Snell's mocking voice brought Judy back into the conversation.

"Village life is rather extraordinary, isn't it?" she said.

77

"Until you're used to it, I suppose. Then you know what to believe and what to—discard."

Mrs Frost changed the conversation, but almost at once Miss Snell got up to go. She reminded the Frosts, in case they had forgotten, that an exhibition of her work would be on in Stourfield for the whole of the next week. She left a small printed notice to this effect on their hall table. After she had passed out of sight up the lane Judy went in again, tore up the notice and threw it into the wastepaper-basket.

"What a frightful woman!" she said.

"She can't help her appearance," Mrs Frost said, mildly. "It's fashionable in those circles not to wash, I believe. At least she doesn't dress in heavy sweaters and knee-high boots. I've seen her about quite often and wondered who she was."

"I shouldn't think her painting's much good," Judy grumbled.

"We can't know that. She's awkward and tactless, but then she came with a purpose and that's always embarrassing for everyone."

"To boost her silly exhibition, you mean?"

"Oh no, to warn you off Julian Farnham."

Judy turned away. The last thing she wanted just then was to discuss Julian with her mother. She went to the telephone and arranged with Susan Singleton, also at home for the weekend, to meet the next morning for a shopping expedition to Stourfield.

Though the whole object of this exercise was to discover all that Susan knew of Julian's relationship with Olivia, Judy could not bring herself to start on this topic until they were driving back to Upfold. Then, in desperation, with only minutes left before it would be too late, she asked quite bluntly if Olivia was engaged to Julian or—something, she added.

"Something," said Susan, pleasantly. "More than some-thing a couple of years ago. But I rather gather it's faded.

Why d'you ask? I thought you'd been seeing a good deal of Julian lately.

"I've only known him just over a week," Judy protested. "I've met him in London exactly twice."

"I call that very good going—for Julian. Why d'you want to know about Olivia?"

"We had Miss Snell—Mabel—round yesterday. Rather a nasty piece of work, I thought. Is the vague, arty manner put on or genuine?"

"Oh, quite genuine. And she's not so old. When she first came here she'd only just left an art school in Paris. Parents had died and left her badly off so she could only scrape along in the country and no more art school. Or that's the tale. I wouldn't know. I was too young. Mummy was kind to her so she often came to meals. Mummy adores lame dogs. It's a kind of vice."

"Surely not?"

"Oh yes. Because when a new one turns up she drops the last one and they resent it."

"I see."

"But Mabel managed to stick, in a way. We went on seeing her, I know, until she began to spread beastly tittle-tattle about Celia Wainwright."

Judy drew in a breath.

"So that was it? She really did have a thing about Julian and took it out on Celia for reasons of jealousy."

"You sound like a popular newspaper. But it's true, I think. She was desperately jealous. Before Celia came here and Julian fell for her in a very big way Mabel thought he'd marry her."

"But he was simply existing on his prizes and army savings. He wouldn't have thought of marrying *anyone*."

Susan said nothing until she had stopped the car outside Mulberry Cottage. Then she turned to Judy and said, "if you know all that why not ask Julian himself about Olivia? If it's important."

79

"It might be. She is—or was—the latest, was she? There would be others—since Celia, I mean."

"I wouldn't know." Susan's voice lost its tone of amusement, grew cold. "I don't take any deep interest in J. Farnham's love life. Olivia happens to be a business friend of mine. We work in the same shop. I have her down for the odd weekend. She's fairly ambitious. She made a mistake over Julian, I think. He's more than a match for her in general self-interest."

"I'm sorry," Judy said, stiffly, opening the car door. "I didn't mean to be a bore. It was the way that Snell woman—"

"Don't take any notice of her," Susan answered, returning to her former warm friendliness. "Cattiness is catching. Look at me, just now."

They parted with good feelings restored between them. Judy went into the house trying to believe she had not given away too blatantly her growing involvement with the person and problems of Julian Farnham.

It was doubly upsetting, therefore, when he rang her up directly after lunch, to ask her to go out with him that afternoon.

"I'm sorry," she said, trying to keep her voice steady. "I can't, I'm afraid."

"Why not?"

Really the arrogance! She repeated her polite refusal.

"You still haven't said why not. Are you booked already?"

Being a truthful girl and aware, against her will, that she had to be honest with this man, she said, "No."

"Have you promised to help your parents with some desperately urgent task at home?"

A laugh rose in her throat but she suppressed it and repeated her denial.

"O.K. I'll be round for you in twenty minutes. Bring a coat. We may be back late."

Judy was thoroughly affronted. Her training and her job allowed her a certain authority. She was used to being given general directions about the patients she helped to rehabilitate. She was not used to orders. In fact, she gave them herself to the juniors and students in her department. So Julian's assumption quite took her breath away, even to the extent of sending her to her mother to explain his extraordinary conduct and demand protection.

"You open the door when he comes," she said. "Tell him I've gone out."

"I'll do no such thing," Mrs Frost said, smiling. "You can manage your own boy-friends. Besides, you know you want to find out just how bad he is, after Miss Snell's gossip yesterday. Go and find out from the man himself."

Judy stared at her mother in astonishment. The latter said, with complete seriousness now, "We need to know, Judy. There's something wrong in Upfold that ought to be put right. Your father means to get to the bottom of it, bless him. You can help if you will, and maybe help Mr Farnham into the bargain."

Judy left her mother and went into the garden. She had no intention of changing from the summer dress and cardigan she had worn to go shopping that morning. She was not going to open the door when Julian arrived.

But he did not go to the door. He sat in the car and pressed the horn. When he had done this twice Dr Frost, who was in the garden near the gate, walked over to the hedge.

"Oh, it's you," he said. "D'you want Judy?"

"Yes," said Julian. "She's coming out with me."

Dr Frost called and Judy came round the corner of the house. Retreat was now impossible, so she continued to advance. Julian got out of the car to open the door for her.

"I'm glad you haven't dolled up," he said, "because I want us to go for a walk on the downs, if that's agreeable."

"Do I have a choice?" she said in a low voice, not moving to the car.

"Don't be silly," he answered, equally low and added in a louder tone, "you'll need a coat, though."

"Is it in the hall cupboard?" Dr Frost asked. "I'll get it."

Cursing both her parents Judy climbed into the passenger seat and fastened the safety belt. Dr Frost brought the mackintosh, handed it in through the open window and stepping back, waved goodbye. Julian drove away, heading south as he had done on their first drive together.

The girl sat rigidly beside him, staring at the road ahead, not answering any of his first attempts at conversation. At last he said, in a low, sad voice, "For God's sake don't shut yourself away like this. D'you think I'd have insisted on this drive if it wasn't desperate? If *I* wasn't desperate, I mean. You're angry—conventionally affronted. This is a nonsense between you and me. You know it is. Won't you be the endearing lovely self you've shown me ever since we met?"

Judy's anger melted on the instant. An appeal to her compassion never failed. He might be a rake, a wolf, as Miss Snell had hinted, but his words, spoken seriously in his very attractive voice, were irresistible.

"I'm sorry, Julian," she said. "It's only—I mean we hardly know each other—but if you're worried about anything—"

He drew in to the next convenient lay-by, stopped the car and regardless of passing traffic or any other manifestation of the world around them, took her in his arms and kissed her.

"I love you," he said. "It's as simple as that."

Judy struggled to keep her mental and emotional balance and failed.

"I think I love you," she answered. Unable to say any more until he released her again she could only manage to add, "—but—"

"But you've heard the usual bloody slanders and gossip and tittle-tattle of the women of Upfold who have nothing better to do than run down their neighbours."

"No," Judy said, recovering slowly, "it's worse than that. You know it is, Julian."

"Yes. I know it is. What have you heard?"

She spoke up bravely then.

"It's what *you've* heard that matters, isn't it? I mean, you knew before that *I'd* heard about you and Celia Wainwright. You practically told me you'd had an affair with her."

"Yes, I did."

She took it as a double confession as he intended she should.

"Well, that was over ten years ago. Your private life is your own affair—"

He groaned.

"Skip the clichés, for God's sake! You don't give a damn for Celia. Why should you? But you're being stuffy all the same. Why?"

"Because you seem not to give a damn for her, either. It was something important and then she ran out on you. Or didn't she? Or don't you know?"

He drew away from her, inclined to be resentful. He had hoped she would accuse him of Celia's successors but she had swung back to the turning point of that affair. His memory of the last night with Celia and its horrible culmination almost overwhelmed him. He struggled to turn from it.

"Really you're jealous of Olivia. That's it, really, isn't it?"

Judy, who had felt she was on the edge of truth, was not going to be led away from it now.

"I was jealous when that awful old Snell began making beastly insinuations," she said. "I was still jealous this morning when I talked to Susan about it. That was why I didn't want to come out with you. Now I don't believe it was very serious, was it? Perhaps you haven't taken anyone very seriously since Celia."

He knew then that he could not escape back into triviality as he had done for so many years. The realisation both exalted and terrified him. To gain time he took Judy into his arms again. She let him kiss her; she returned his passion with an ardour of her own she had never felt before. But she would not be turned from her purpose.

"You *must* tell me," she implored. "Did she run out on you?"

"No. At least—no, she definitely didn't *run* out."

"Did she go away with you that night?"

"No."

"But you knew where she'd gone when everyone thought she'd disappeared?"

"No. I did not."

Judy paused. News of the so-called hoax had been circulated throughout the village. It was impossible that Julian, who frequented the local pub, had not heard of it. She went on, cautiously, "You must have heard of Daddy's find. In the old hen-run?"

He looked at her, puzzled by this sudden switch.

"D'you mean the famous hoax? I've heard something—village lads having fun—"

"The hoax was *not* fun. The find was genuine."

She saw his face whiten and her heart sank.

"I ought not to tell you this. I'm doing so to help you to tell me what you've kept secret so long. Daddy found *real* bones and he kept some of them and took them to a pathologist. I think they will turn out to be Celia Wainwright."

"My *God*!" he whispered. "So that—"

He broke off, staring at Judy, bewilderment and fear in his eyes, turning at last to anger.

"No," Judy said, moving closer to him again. "You mustn't —Only tell me—"

But he shook her off, started the engine and drove away towards the downs without another word. Judy, conscious only of failure and bitter disillusion, shrank miserably against her seat, longing only for the drive to come to an end.

CHAPTER VIII

By the time they reached the hotel where they had dinner both Julian and Judy had recovered, if not their spirits, at least a full command of their emotions. Their main attraction for one another was the ease they each felt in the other's presence. This did not fail them now and on the whole, at a rather superficial level, the expedition was quite a success. Judy's sudden fear of him in the car left her entirely as they walked on the downs. Their talk was chiefly an exchange of autobiography, fascinating to hear, delightful to impart. When they reached Mulberry Cottage again Judy had recovered enough to say, quietly, "Won't you come in and talk to Daddy? Don't you think you ought to?"

He gave a short, disagreeable laugh.

"So that's it, is it? Still digging for the evidence? Haven't you done enough, you and your father, one way or another?"

"That isn't fair! You know it isn't like that!"

"Do I? Listen, my girl. If you think I buried Celia Wainwright in her own hen-run, you're not only wrong, you're crazy. And now will you get out of my car and let me go home? Or have you planned a confrontation, don't they call it, at the site of my supposed crime?"

Judy was both shocked and hurt, but she kept her head.

"Don't be ridiculous," she said, getting briskly out of the car, but standing outside the closed door to look in at him. "Thank you for the ride—and everything—my darling."

He swore at her and drove off so suddenly that she had to jump back to avoid being dashed to the ground.

Nothing had been said about their meeting again and Judy went back to London the following evening feeling sad, puzzled and inclined to blame herself for the present hitch in a promising and much-desired relationship. She determined, nevertheless, to get to the bottom of the strange affair that had come between her and her lover. With this in mind she went over all the facts and rumours she had heard from her parents and decided that the strangest and also the one most easily gone into was the drowning of the butcher's little boy.

So on the following Saturday, having gone down to Upfold for yet another weekend, she went boldly into the offices of the *Stourfield Gazette*, a weekly publication, and asked for permission to look up some entries for the year 1953. After some delay and not a few strange looks she found herself seated at a wide table with a number of very large volumes in red leather bindings that held copies of every edition of the *Gazette* for the whole of that year.

Faced with a task much greater than she had anticipated, Judy cursed herself for not asking in which month the accident had taken place. But she knew that Mrs Wainwright had disappeared in the autumn of the year and that the Pawley child had fallen in the river while playing near it. This might, of course, have been at any time, but was perhaps more likely in the summer than in the winter. So starting from the end of September she worked back through the year until she came upon the inquest, which had taken place early in April. The main facts of the drowning were set out here in full and made very strange reading.

Celia Wainwright had been the only adult at the scene of the accident when it happened. She saw the little boy step backward off the bank and fall in the water. She sent the other children to run for help and herself found a long stick very quickly and held it out to the child. But he was too frightened to understand what she wanted him to do. If he had grasped the stick she could have pulled him to safety but he did not. She could not swim. She knew the water was very deep at that spot.

Only one of the children, a boy of ten, Richard Winter, gave evidence. What he said caused such a sensation in the coroner's court that order had to be restored by the police and several people removed. The boy told how he and his younger friends had been playing together when Mrs Wainwright came on the scene. She had stopped to speak to them, but they were frightened of her and told her to go away. She did not go, but she stared at Roy Pawley and made him walk back into the water. She took a stick and poked him under.

The coroner had intervened to dispute this interpretation, asking why Mrs Wainwright should wish to harm anyone.

"Because she be a witch," the boy answered.

"Was that why you asked her to go away?"

"Ay, it were. We be afeared of 'un."

Mrs Wainwright was recalled and asked about the behaviour of the children. She then said they had called her names and had begun to throw stones at her. Little Roy Pawley had thrown a stone and overbalanced into the water in doing so. Asked why she had not said this before she explained that she had not wished to distress the parents. It was then that the uproar broke out.

The coroner had found death to be due to misadventure. He complimented Mrs Wainwright upon her efforts to save the child. He spoke severely about superstition and said that it was both wrong and cruel to put such dreadful ideas into young children's heads. Superstition and ignorance of this sort were a survival from the middle ages that had no place in modern life. The reporter noted that his words were received in a hostile silence and that Mrs Wainwright left the court by a side door with an escort of police to see her to her husband's car.

Richard Winter. Judy wrote down the name in her diary and showed it to her parents when she got back to Mulberry Cottage.

"I wonder if he's a relation of the Mrs Winter who does our laundry," her mother said. "We can find out, of course."

"Better not make a thing of it," Dr Frost advised.

"No," his wife answered. "I'll wait till Monday. I generally collect from her now and take the new lot down with me. Mr Winter never calls when I'm in and I don't like to have it lying on the doorstep and perhaps getting rained on."

"You do that," Judy said. She went on, "Those other children. The ones that ran for help or ran away. One of them was a brother of the little boy."

"Pawley," said Dr Frost. "Pawley, the butcher. He has a son at the grammar school in Stourfield. Doing very well, they say. Scholarship to one of the midland universities."

"Leeds," said Mrs Frost.

Judy looked with admiration from one to the other of her parents.

"Proper old village gossips, aren't you?" she said. "How do we get in touch with this young Pawley? He must be about eighteen, I suppose? That would be right for age. Eight in 1953. The younger child was six. How can we get hold of the Pawley boy?"

Dr Frost looked blank. Mrs Frost said, briskly, "You can come and help me with the teas at the Club this afternoon. I promised Mrs Marshall I'd go along about four. The Sports Club," she added, seeing the others continued to look blank. "Cricket, at present. The Pawley family are very keen. Mr Pawley umpires. Upfold have a very good eleven, this year. They beat a Stourfield team last Saturday."

Remembering how her last weekend was spent Judy was not surprised at her ignorance of this event. Dr Frost said, "Yes, go and help your mother. I knew she'd be roped into all sorts of things. You can at least lighten her burden."

"I like meeting people," Mrs Frost protested.

"What about my tea?" Dr Frost asked her.

"You can come down as well. The Club will stand you a cup of tea and a biscuit, I'm sure."

Dr Frost groaned but made no further complaint. He had one or two odd jobs to do in the garden, but he thought he might stroll down to the village green later.

The Pawley family was there in force, as usual, Mr Pawley in the long white coat of an umpire; Mrs Pawley in the pavilion behind the tea cups; some daughters watching the match with friends. Sitting on the grass, waiting for his turn to bat, was a slim young version of Mr Pawley, with the same dark hair and eyes and gypsy complexion.

Mrs Frost pointed out the various members of the butcher's family to Judy as they walked over to the pavilion. Inside she introduced her to Mrs Pawley and stationed her at the latter's side to help with pouring out the tea.

"My girls usually do it," Mrs Pawley said. "But Steve's playing today and they're all set to watch him bat. Not but what he'll be out first ball, I wouldn't wonder. Cricket doesn't really suit him. Too slow, he always says. Tennis is more his game."

Judy entered on a long, if intermittent discussion of various games and sports, including those suitable or not suitable for girls. She refrained from any mention of swimming or boating.

At the interval there was no time for conversation of any kind. Though the number of spectators Judy and her mother had passed on their way along the field to the pavilion had been insignificant in that green expanse, with its cluster of white figures at the centre, the whole village and a large number of strangers as well seemed to have gathered during the last hour or so.

Judy worked hard. Mrs Pawley was gratified. When there was a pause in the rush for tea she said, "I'd like my girls to watch you. You're a real worker, Miss Frost."

"Oh, I *am*," said Judy. "You should see me on a Monday morning in the department of the hospital where I work."

Stephen Pawley came across to his mother.

"Out for a duck, as usual," he said, cheerfully. "Dad isn't half mad at me."

"Bad luck," Judy said. Mrs Pawley introduced her son. She handed a cup of tea to Judy.

"You've done your bit," she said. "There won't be much more now. Take your tea outside. Steve, Miss Frost's keen on sport. Show her round the pavilion if it isn't too crowded. It's new," she added.

"Three years ago, it was," her son corrected.

"Three years is new in Upfold," argued Mrs Pawley.

They all laughed and Judy moved away, her heart beating with excitement. This was lucky, indeed. She wouldn't be able to keep the boy talking long but with a few careful questions she might get what she wanted.

It was comparatively easy. Steve took up his mother's hint that Miss Frost liked sport. He found her knowledgeable on most games and enthusiastic for lacrosse which he had never seen played but was interested to hear about. Judy led him on to swimming and water sports. He spoke quite naturally of them; he had mastered the crawl and could dive reasonably well.

"I don't let on much about this at home," he said, looking at her with an inquiring eye.

"I suppose not," said Judy, nodding to show she understood.

It was the desired opening and she made proper use of it. Steve, quite unsuspecting, talked freely about the accident to his little brother. It had been the kid's own fault, he said. Poor little blighter, he'd been too scared of Mrs Wainwright to do what she shouted to him. Come to that, he wouldn't have fallen in if he hadn't been so excited throwing stones at her. When she told him to stop he'd begun to be frightened and stepped back without looking, straight into the river.

"A child of that age, throwing stones, meaning to hurt!" Judy said. She was profoundly shocked.

"We all were. We thought she was a witch."

Judy stared.

"You really and truly thought that? Who put the idea into your heads?"

Steve pushed a hand through his hair.

"I dunno. Everyone was saying it. Actually Mum and Dad still think so. Crazy, isn't it? I mean, in this day and age—"

His face had grown very red.

"I entirely agree with you," Judy said, stoutly. "To me it's incredible. I can understand little children being frightened of witches, believing there are witches, but not grown-up people. Did you yourself honestly think poor Mrs Wainwright was a witch?"

"I don't really know. I was eight when Roy fell in the river. I think I was more frightened of what Mum would say to me for not looking after him. I never thought he'd be dead. I just ran for help and I remember thinking I'd have to get him dried off before I took him home."

"Yes. I can understand all that perfectly. You probably thought he was a bit of a nuisance anyway, when you wanted to play with people your own age."

"That's right. I did. He was very excitable."

"Easily frightened. Poor kid!"

The thought of little Roy, terrified of the witch, refusing to catch hold of the saving stick because an evil being held it, sickened her. His imagination, his atavistic fears, had been falsely fed by those who should have known better.

"You didn't give evidence at the inquest, did you?" she asked.

"No. They didn't like to ask me to, Mum says now. I don't remember any of that myself."

"Only Richard Winter gave evidence."

"That's right." Steve looked at Judy, puzzled by her insistence. "How d'you know all this? What's the idea?"

"It's this witch business," Judy said, truthfully. "Mrs Wainwright lived in our house so I'm curious about her. We've been told all the legends—"

"*All?*"

Steve gave her a quizzical look, far older than his reputed years. Judy found herself blushing.

"How should I know?" she said, with a rather artificial

laugh. "Anyway, your generation in Upfold have discarded the witch theory, I take it?"

"Most of us," Steve answered with a smile. "Except Dick Winter, of course."

"Why of course?"

"Haven't you come across his old granny yet? Ma Cowley. Granma Cowley she is, really. There's a witch for you, if you're looking for one."

They had been standing at the edge of the field and now Judy saw arms waving in their direction.

"I think you're wanted," she said. "Yes, they're going out again."

"Wish me luck with the bowling," Steve said, cheerfully, beginning to pull off his sweater as he moved away.

A nice boy, Judy thought, carrying her cup back to the pavilion. Easy to talk to, no chips on those good broad shoulders. And why should there be, with the butcher supplying the neighbourhood for miles round and the weekenders all wanting home-killed meat and thinking they got it cheaper than in London? A prosperous home, a large car, summer holidays on the continent. That was the Pawleys.

"What a very nice boy Stephen is," she said to Mrs Pawley who was packing the crockery into big crates.

The mother responded warmly, but with reservations.

"Oh yes, he's a good lad. Clever, though I say so. Too scientific for us, I'm afraid. He *will* argue with Dad and you know what that means."

Judy did not, because discussion was more usual than argument in her home, but she nodded agreement just the same. She knew what the argument would be about. A modern outlook on the one hand, a medieval one on the other. Inquiry versus established belief. An open mind versus superstition. And such superstition!

Having helped Mrs Pawley again until the work was finished Judy went out to find her parents and to watch Steve Pawley bowling. The Upfold side had been all out for ninety-seven, but their opponents had already lost two wickets for only fifteen, so things looked quite bright for the home side.

The Frosts left the field before the close of play and returned to Mulberry Cottage. Judy was half hoping to find some message from Julian pushed into the letter-box. But it was empty. He had not appeared at the cricket ground, no one there had mentioned his name to her. In fairness she realised that she had not given anyone much chance to speak to her, except Mrs Pawley and her son.

All the evening and the next day until it was time to catch her train Judy waited for the phone call or the message, or best of all, the appearance of the man who now occupied the centre of her mind. But nothing happened. She had come home that weekend determined to settle what she felt and thought about Julian. She had settled nothing—discovered— what? That an intelligent boy did not accept a fantastic legend. So what? So what, indeed!

Mrs Frost, on the other hand, carried her parcel of laundry to Mrs Winter's house full of determination to discover more about the boy Richard. Two facts Dr Frost had picked up at the cricket match. One, that Richard was indeed the son of their Mrs Winter. And the second, that he worked for George Cutfield as a farm labourer. So Dr Frost argued, he might have had access to Jim Cutfield's anatomy school bones.

The Winters lived at the end of a lane near the church. Most of the cottages there were small and old-fashioned, standing in pairs with narrow front gardens and small vegetable plots at the back. The Winter's cottage, however, stood alone and was remarkable for the wealth of flowers blooming in the front garden. There was no grass plot there as there was in most of the others. The flowers, hollyhocks, foxgloves, daisies, poppies and many shorter plants, without flowers, that Mrs Frost did not recognise, all stood in thick clumps, filling the air with scents and the sound of bees.

Mrs Frost was greeted with pleasure and apologies.

"My 'usband do go on so over delivering the washing," Mrs Winters explained. It was her favourite lament. "You can see for why. 'E's out in the fields all day and looks to rest 'is legs when 'e come 'ome."

"Naturally," said Mrs Frost. "And I've plenty of time on my hands now that my husband has retired, so I'll go on being my own laundry van in future, shall I? Call on Monday with the dirty washing and fetch away the clean."

"If it won't be an imposition, m'm," said Mrs Winter, smiling broadly.

"Of course not."

"Then I'll just make up your parcel if you'll step indoors a minute."

This Mrs Frost was only too pleased to do. As a mark of particular favour and friendship Mrs Winter took her into the big airy kitchen from where a huge copper was visible in the scullery beyond, already heating up for the week's wash. The large scrubbed table was covered with freshly-ironed clothes and linen, sorted into neat piles. Everything about the room was clean and shining, the crockery on the big dresser, the pots and pans above the wide modern cooking stove, the cupboards, the sink. Everything except the twisted figure of an old woman, bent into an armchair near the window.

Mrs Frost recoiled a little from the sight. The figure was dressed in black, a rusty black that showed up the grease spots and traces of spilt food on her bodice and in her lap. Her hair was black with only a white streak here and there, dusty and stringy for want of washing. The face was heavily lined, grey with dirt in the creases, yellow about the mouth where a trembling hand continually wiped away a film of spittle.

"Gran," said Mrs Winter loudly, as Mrs Frost stared at this incongruous sight. "This is Mrs Frost, come for 'er washing." Turning to the latter, she added in a lower voice, "She's deaf, but not so deaf as she make out. We leaves 'er

94

be, you understand. She be that obstinate, you'd 'ardly credit, though I'm 'er daughter as says so."

"You will be Mrs Cowley," said Mrs Frost, in a kindly voice, forcing herself to approach the old woman's chair, though an increasingly evil smell held her some distance away.

"I'm Mrs Cowley," the old woman said. "You're new 'ere, Mrs Frost, bain't you?"

"You see. She 'eard all right," Mrs Winter whispered.

"Never mind what *she* says," Mrs Cowley went on, twisting herself round still further to get a good look at Mrs Frost. "So you've brought your own washing along, 'ave you? Too proud to do it yourself, I suppose?"

The words were foolish and trivial, but the malice that prompted them was so strong and so apparent that Mrs Frost caught her breath.

"I've 'eard tell there was new folks at Mulberry," the old woman went on. "It's bin empty these ten year and no wonder. *She's* seen to that."

"Who do you mean by *she?*" Mrs Frost asked steadily.

Mrs Cowley gave a low chuckle of delight.

"As if you didn't know," she said. "As if you 'adn't knowed all along."

"Now, mother," Mrs Winter began, feebly, but Mrs Cowley beat the arm of her chair with a grimy hand.

"Get along with you, Elsie. The lady's 'ere to fetch 'er washing, isn't she, and it not done up ready, yet."

Mrs Winter retreated to the far end of the big table and began to check the Frosts' list.

Mrs Frost said, firmly, "Well, of course we've heard all sorts of silly stories about witchcraft and that sort of nonsense. We don't believe in these tales. In fact we think whoever spread them in the first place was spreading a wicked slander about poor Mrs Wainwright."

Mrs Cowley took this in silence. Perhaps she did not hear it, or not all of it. Mrs Frost watched and waited. Presently

95

Mrs Cowley's small eyes glinted sideways at her and without turning her face she spoke to the whole room.

"The Wainwright woman 'ad the power. I seen it afore when I were a young girl. A woman, too. Fine and 'andsome as she. There were death following of 'er and suicide, like she brought to Thompson's lad. Devil's work. I'm not the only one that see it."

"Wicked rubbish!" cried Mrs Frost, thoroughly roused by the other's manner, the relish and suppressed glee with which she spoke. "You drove Mrs Wainwright away. Perhaps to suicide, herself."

She was thinking, in a muddled way, of the bones in the hen-run.

"And wot if she did?" Mrs Cowley declared. "They gain power if they takes their own lives. The evil spirit is free for more devil's work, unless they be buried—"

"Here's your parcel," said Mrs Winter loudly, coming forward. She added, rather breathlessly, "You don't 'ave to listen to 'er, m'm. Gran wanders a bit in 'er mind these days."

But Mrs Frost was past caring what anyone said to her.

"You invented all this!" she accused. "Why? Why did you spread this wicked nonsense? You have a lot to answer for. You corrupted the children! You're the one responsible for—"

She was on the point of saying "for the Pawley child's death", but she stopped herself, frightened and distressed by her own outburst.

But Mrs Cowley was not at all abashed. A happy grin spread slowly over her face during Mrs Frost's speech, until it absorbed and obliterated all other expression, even in her eyes. She chuckled again, delighted with the effect she had made.

"Nay, my girl," she said. "It warn't me that started it. I were told. On good authority. By one as should know." Her glee increased; she rocked from side to side in her evil mirth. "Oh my Lord, one as should know. That's good, that is! One as should know!"

CHAPTER IX

Towards the end of that week Dr Frost had a letter from Dr Wallace, enclosing a copy of his report on the bones submitted to him for examination. This confirmed the opinion Dr Frost already held.

The bones belonged to a young woman in her middle twenties. There was an old fracture of the clavicle, well mended; the injuries to the sternum and ribs could have been made by the wooden stake. Traces of blood had been found on the wood and the bones and on the former a few minute fragments of heart muscle that had survived decomposition. This suggested that the stake had been driven through the body. If that was so the burial would appear to be one of ancient ritual, based on the superstition that a witch might exercise enhanced powers after death unless so dealt with. A suicide, too, required this treatment, otherwise the self-destroyed, being damned eternally and under the power of the devil, might exercise witchcraft after death.

Dr Wallace set out these explanations in full. Evidently he found the case of absorbing interest from an atavistic, sociological point of view. In his letter he said that he had reported the facts to Scotland Yard and to the Director of Public Prosecutions. The former had notified the county C.I.D. at Stourfield and had begun to make some inquiries. Their difficulty, Dr Wallace pointed out, was firstly that the remains could not be identified with certainty as those of Mrs Wainwright and secondly that there was no confirmation whatever of her alleged disappearance. On the other hand there was no doubt that some interested party or parties in Upfold had deliberately taken away the rest of the discovered skeleton from the tool-shed. The local police were going into that and would no doubt get in touch with Dr Frost shortly.

As they had not already done so the doctor drove into Stourfield, taking Dr Wallace's letter and report with him. He found that a Detective-Chief-Inspector Falk, of the county C.I.D. was in charge of the case.

Falk was in when Dr Frost arrived and greeted him without marked cordiality. He glanced at the report briefly, handed it back and said, "We've got a copy." When he had read Dr Wallace's letter he handed that back too, without comment.

"I thought it would save time if I came in to see you rather than the other way about," Dr Frost said, quietly.

"Save time over what, sir? Seeing the bones are ten years old, time doesn't appear to come into it."

"Perhaps not."

Though Dr Frost was prepared to allow for a certain lack of enthusiasm, he had not expected hostility.

"Perhaps not," he repeated. "They would destroy the rest of the bones as soon as they got hold of them. I don't see how we can ever get at the truth of that."

"Meaning by 'they'?"

"Whoever arranged the substitution." Dr Frost was becoming annoyed. "Haven't you found who they were yet? It should not be too difficult. I told no one but the constable's wife that I wanted to see her husband. I was away from home only just over three hours. But in that time Jim Cutfield's set of bones and Dr Marshall's set were stolen and put in my shed and the others removed. Cutfield's set was probably taken by Dick Winter who works at the farm. His old grandmother seems to be primarily responsible for the fantastic legend of witchcraft at Upfold."

Inspector Falk listened to all this with growing indignation.

No one had put him wise to this gaffer. A silly old man who'd had a hoax played on him, had been the starting point of his own inquiries. This request from the Yard for details of the hoax had only come in that morning. He had not yet studied it carefully. Dr Frost's summing up of the facts took him aback. The old man was very far from senile. In fact he knew a lot too much.

"I should like to know, doctor," Falk said, stiffly, "how you come by all that information and why you did not see fit to notify us of it?"

"I was waiting to hear from Wallace," said Dr Frost, not at all disturbed by the other's severity. "I happened to know young Cutfield was at St Edmund's. My hospital and Wallace's. I spoke to him there. He told me his bones were at the farm. Dr Marshall I've met at Upfold, naturally. He found his bones had been stolen too."

"Borrowed, you might call it," Inspector Falk said, defensively. "Galton soon found it was young Winter who'd taken the set at the farm. They've been handed back. Same with Dr Marshall as soon as he notified Galton they were missing."

"Who took them?"

"That was more of a problem. Anyone in the house, when the doctor was out. He doesn't keep his surgery door locked."

"There can't be many people in the house. Only his wife and any domestic help they have."

"It's not quite as easy as that, sir. The waiting room for the surgery has an outside door into the road and an inside door into the surgery. Anyone who could borrow the outside key could get into the surgery without being noticed by the people in the house."

"But the whole thing was arranged in less than three hours!"

"Dr Marshall had a surgery that afternoon. It was a short one, over before four. He locked the outer door as usual at the end of it."

"On the inside? The key was on the inside?"

99

"Yes."

"Then whoever took the bones must have been in the house to start with."

"That's right. She was."

"Who did it?"

"Mrs Thompson. Daily. She denies it, but I'm pretty sure she's the one. You know her, I see."

Dr Frost nodded.

"I know her. She works for us, too. She worked for the Wainwrights and she believes that Mrs Wainwright destroyed her son."

Falk looked uncomfortable.

"The boy that committed suicide when he failed his exam? Yes, I heard of that. She didn't refer to it when I saw her about the bones."

"The bones—yes. I suppose she took the key before she left, went in by the waiting room, got the bones, went out by the same door, leaving it unlocked with the key on the inside and walked off without being seen."

"Yes. Mrs Marshall went into the waiting room later, simply thought the doctor had forgotten to lock up for once and locked the door herself. So he never knew until he discovered his loss and notified us."

"He discovered his loss when I asked him if he'd got a set of bones that could have been used in the so-called hoax," Dr Frost said.

"Oh, yes?" The inspector was not to be drawn.

"What did Mrs Thompson actually say when you accused her of taking them? Deny it outright?"

"Yes. But said the lads were having you on and she saw no harm in it."

"I see."

Dr Frost considered. It was plain to him that Inspector Falk had cleared up what he had taken to be a silly prank to his own entire satisfaction and was considerably put out when he found that much more lay behind it. Put out and definitely resentful. It would be tactful on his own part to retire at this stage. But his curiosity was great and growing.

"I told you just now that Mrs Thompson worked for the Wainwrights. I am wondering if she can throw any light on the disappearance, as they call it in Upfold. Have you asked her?"

"I saw her yesterday evening," Falk said. "As soon as we had this report down from the Yard. I'd cleared up the other business before."

"You didn't tell me," Dr Frost said, reproachfully.

Falk ignored this. The old man would have heard all right. It had depended on whether any charge would be made. They hadn't decided that when this other cropped up.

"Mrs Thompson remembered clearly going to Mulberry Cottage at ten in the morning on the day Mrs Wainwright was—missing. The milk was on the door-step, the newspaper and letters in the box. All untouched. The doors were locked, the curtains drawn in the downstairs rooms. She walked round the house, rang the bells, knocked, got no answer and went away. Mr Wainwright arrived back in his car that afternoon."

"By which time the whole of Upfold knew, or thought they knew, that Mrs Wainwright had gone."

"That's right. Mrs Thompson didn't see him. She kept away, she said."

"Typical. You won't get much from the other village people. Either they believe Mrs Wainwright was a witch or they're ashamed of their elders and betters having such nonsensical ideas."

"They can't really *believe*—what you said?"

Falk could not bring himself to use the word 'witch' in this context.

"Don't they? You find out what they did with the rest of the skeleton and what happened ten years ago to the head. There's no skull in my garden. I won't keep you any longer. I expect I'll be seeing you again. Good-day to you."

Dr Frost walked out of the police station not very much wiser than when he went in. But at least the Yard was taking the matter seriously. When they had established that Mrs Wainwright had indeed disappeared without trace, perhaps the reluctant Chief-Inspector would pull his socks up.

As no further news came to him during the next few days Dr Frost began to fret again. He knew that neither he nor Jeanie would feel happy in Upfold until this strange affair was explained. And, contrary to Falk's implied belief, the doctor felt sure the answer was to be found in the village. Dr Marshall, he rightly concluded, knew more than he had so far revealed, but was unwilling to disclose professional secrets, even to a retired colleague, before he was obliged to. Dr Frost decided to speak to the vicar again. Mr Shalford, also, seemed to know more than he had been willing to reveal.

The vicar was in his study, reading, when Dr Frost called. Mrs Shalford, explaining this, asked the doctor to come in.

"I don't want to disturb him," he said.

"I'd love you to," Mrs Shalford answered. "It's only a new thriller he's reading, that he brought home from the Public Library in Stourfield this morning. He's got two sermons he ought to be writing, for next Sunday matins here and the evening service at Littlefold. If you stop him now I'll get the book away and he'll settle down to work when you leave."

"By which time you'll be deep in the thriller yourself, I suspect," said Dr Frost.

Mrs Shalford laughed. She was an amiable, simple individual, without much intelligence or imagination, Dr Frost decided. Quite incapable of approaching, far less dealing with, the darker side of village life as it was being slowly, too slowly, revealed. He followed her to the vicar's study, feeling that he was wasting a fine afternoon when he might have done some useful hoeing among the weeds now springing up all round his various seedlings.

But Mr Shalford, though vague and inclined to be indolent, was no fool. He grasped immediately the full reason for the doctor's visit and before long had succeeded in getting the bare facts of Dr Frost's discovery. The latter had come prepared to add to his knowledge of the villagers by questioning Mr Shalford. He found himself imparting knowledge instead.

"Well, now you've got the whole story," he said, when the vicar became silent, staring sadly out of the window. "I didn't really intend to give it you at this stage."

"I think, if I am to help you, I need to know all the facts," said Mr Shalford, gently.

"And you read detective stories," said Dr Frost.

Mr Shalford blushed.

"That is not much help in present circumstances, I fear," he answered. "But tell me how do you think I can be of use and I will do my best."

"What d'you know about Mrs Thompson's family?" Dr Frost began. "And the Winters? The old grandmother, for instance? My wife says she's like an old witch herself."

"The Cowleys are of gypsy origin," Mr Shalford said. "In fact, many of the people are. The Pawleys for instance, two generations back on the mother's side. The Cowleys have been settled here for at least four generations. Mrs Winter is the second daughter. Her sister-in-law, the husband's sister, is Mrs Galton, wife of the constable."

"Ah!" Dr Frost was delighted. "So that's how Dick Winter was put on to taking Jim Cutfield's bones at the farm. Now Mrs Thompson. Who's she related to?"

"She's Mrs Galton's sister."

"Too easy, isn't it? And bad luck for the constable, who's not an Upfold man, I gather, and probably only knows what his wife allows him to."

"It's more than likely," sighed the vicar. "Mrs Galton has put a spoke in a good many of poor Galton's attempts to control the village rowdies. Though I must say she was very helpful over the hooligans at the Clubhouse. Put him on the right track there. He was commended by the Superintendent in Stourfield."

Dr Frost felt they were wandering from the reason for his visit.

"You realise, don't you, that if the bones I found are assumed to be those of Celia Wainwright—in other words, if Scotland Yard comes to the conclusion that she has really disappeared—we shall have a murder here to investigate?"

"Or, surely, a suicide?"

"Suicides don't bury themselves in hen-runs without their heads and with a stake driven through their hearts."

The vicar shuddered.

"She was ill, you know," he said, in a low voice. "Physically and mentally, I thought, towards the end."

"Why?"

"Why was she ill? Or why did I think so?"

"Both."

"She looked ill. She had been visiting Marshall. She refused invitations. She stayed at home most of the time. But that was natural."

"Why?"

"Because of the cruel persecution. Oh yes, it amounted to that towards the end. If she went into a shop the other customers, if they were village people, would leave and stand outside until she came out and then go in again. The stores asked her to telephone orders and delivered them because it interrupted their business so much."

"And the greengrocer and the butcher?"

Mr Shalford winced.

"Pawley? Oh he, poor man, was the worst of the lot. Refused to serve the Wainwrights at all. On account of the boy."

"Didn't Wainwright himself do anything about it? She must have told him—complained—"

"I don't know." The vicar looked more uncomfortable

than ever. "She was strange, as I said. We thought her mentally unstable."

"We?"

"My wife and I. She took it all so calmly. She seemed to submit to persecution with an unnatural humility."

"A truly Christian attitude?" Dr Frost could not help suggesting.

The vicar looked offended.

"I'm not blaming her for it, poor girl. She was rather a saint in a way, I thought. But it wasn't natural."

"So we decide there was mental trouble," said Dr Frost, goaded. "Unless people behave with total, primitive *naturalness*—unless they show no restraint, no control, no discrimination, in any of their actions, unless they prove themselves uncivilised, uncultivated barbarians, they must be suffering from some form of mental illness! The modern attitude to behaviour and a lamentable one."

"I entirely agree with you," said Mr Shalford, earnestly. "The people who talked like that—it was those who ought to have known better, like Miss Snell—"

"Oh, yes," Dr Frost interrupted. "Miss Snell. It would be Miss Snell."

"And Mrs Graveney, who always talked about 'poor Celia' as if she had cancer or something."

"Perhaps she had," said Dr Frost, "though I think it was something more inevitably deadly, myself."

"Is there?"

"More *immediately* inevitably deadly," the doctor amended. He went on, trying to discover something specific from the vicar's ramblings. "Can you think of anything besides the tragedies of Pawley's child and Mrs Thompson's son that was laid at her door? As due to her supernatural powers?"

"There was the dog that worried Cutfield's sheep," said Mr Shalford, after considerable thought.

"Her dog?"

"Well, yes and no. They had a dog and it did give trouble. But Wainwright had it put down."

"I know. Winter told us."

"This was another dog. The trouble was it turned up from nowhere, they said. It wasn't recognised by anyone in the village."

"A strange dog? A stray, on the loose, looking for food?"

"That was the rational explanation. Galton wasn't here then. His predecessor was elderly and stout. Didn't care for turning out at night to watch. Cutfield did, though, several times, and *they never saw a dog at all.*"

"They?"

"Pawley usually went with him. Friends from schooldays onwards."

"Cutfield doesn't strike me as a superstitious type."

"He isn't. It was Pawley decided the dog was Celia in were-wolf form."

"Appalling!" exclaimed Dr Frost. "Horrible and revolting! Seriously? He thought this *seriously?*"

"I argued with him many times," said Mr Shalford sadly. "With him and with Mrs Cowley and young Dick Winters, before the inquest on poor little Roy. No good. I couldn't move them."

"Couldn't you have run an exorcism parade or something?" suggested Dr Frost. "Met their superstition with a counter-blast of the same."

In his early days he had found the bottle of tinted, orange-flavoured water wholly successful in dealing with medical superstition, but he had spoken now without thinking in whose presence he was. Mr Shalford's face went quite white and though he kept his gentle voice and good manners it was plain that the interview was at an end and that there was little likelihood of others of the kind taking place at any future date.

"I'm sorry," Dr Frost apologised. "I spoke without thinking. But the devil, you know—One can't really believe—"

"The devil has been abroad in Upfold for many years," said Mr Shalford firmly. "I believe that and I shall continue to believe it. My ministry here has been—er—bedevilled—literally."

On this note they parted, Dr Frost indignant, the vicar saddened by the thought of yet another recruit to the ranks of local unbelievers. But Dr Frost, unlike the vicar, was by no means defeated. After telling his wife in detail about his argument with the Church, he went, with her approval, to see the butcher.

Mr Pawley was quite willing to talk to him but told him absolutely nothing. He took Dr Frost into a pleasant sitting room behind the shop and there, looking out over a wide yard with the wall of an abbatoir at the end of it, the two men talked all round the subject of Mrs Wainwright, the hoax in the tool-shed, the police inquiries and finally, the Pawley family tragedy.

But Dr Frost got nowhere. Mr Pawley stated firmly and baldly that Mrs Wainwright had murdered his son and bewitched the coroner. Nothing that the doctor suggested moved him one fraction from this position.

But when Dr Frost got home again he went at once to the telephone to ring up Inspector Falk and having by good luck found him at the police station said, "I thought you might like to know that Pawley, the butcher here—you remember his trouble—"

"The child that drowned. Yes, yes."

"Pawley has his own small slaughter house to deal with local produce. In the yard behind it he has a fair-sized, modern incinerator. If he hasn't used the place for slaughter since I found the bones, I suggest you have a look at the ash in it—if any. Dr Wallace would be happy, I know, to investigate any specimens of any kind you might discover there. I didn't, of course, tell Pawley I knew my skeleton was a real find."

"Thank you, doctor," Falk said. "As a matter of fact I

sent a chap along yesterday with a tale about inspecting the abbattoir. They hadn't killed anything there for over a week. The incinerator was as clean as a whistle."

"They keep a jump ahead of us, don't they?" said Dr Frost.

"It's the grape-vine," said Falk, sadly.

CHAPTER X

Dr Frost reported his latest news to Dr Wallace but the latter had no comfort for him. Scotland Yard had made contact with old Mr Wainwright through the local police at Trethuan in Cornwall, where he had gone to live after his retirement from business. Mr Wainwright had nothing to offer them. He believed that his wife, Celia, had deserted him. She had left no message at Mulberry Cottage when she went away. He had no idea where she had gone. His efforts to trace her had all failed. She had not gone to any of her known London friends. She had no relatives in this country. Letters to her parents in Australia had been returned marked, 'Gone away. Address unknown.' His own opinion was that she had committed suicide, after leaving him, perhaps in some river where her body had remained hidden; or in some wood where no one had found it. She was taking sedative pills at the time of her disappearance. She had the means to hand for suicide. It was on this assumption that he had married again.

"There's a second Mrs Wainwright," Dr Frost told his wife.

"Indeed? He seems to have been pretty sure Celia was dead, doesn't he?"

"With no news of her at all it was a fair assumption."

"Did he really try very hard to find her? Did he get in the police?"

"I gather not. But he made inquiries. He thought at first she'd gone off with Julian."

"As most people here did. I must say it's very fishy his concluding on no evidence at all that he was free to marry again."

"It's been done before. Many times. With no sinister implications. Perhaps he employed a private detective. The sort of person who gathers evidence for divorce. He would, I think, if he had his eye on Julian."

Mrs Frost nodded.

"With the idea of divorcing her? Yes. Perhaps he did. Perhaps her tracks just faded. And Julian came back here, alone, didn't he? After staying with friends. Or so he says."

"There can't have been any tracks," her husband reminded her. "Celia never left Upfold."

"No more she did. I'm getting as muddled as the police seem to be over this. The answer is here, in the village, isn't it?"

"I'm perfectly certain it is."

So Mrs Frost decided to go to work on the local women. By this time it was common knowledge in Upfold that the hoax had been no hoax at all. Mrs Galton agreed that after taking Dr Frost's message she had got in touch with her sister-in-law, Mrs Winter, by sending one of her children down the village street with a note.

Mrs Galton did not agree that she had invented the plan of the substitution, even that she had guessed the nature of Dr Frost's find in the hen-run. Mrs Frost knew it would be no good asking Mrs Galton outright what she knew about the Wainwright mystery. But all the same it was a curious thing for Mrs Galton to have done.

"My husband didn't tell you it was bones he'd found, did he?"

Mrs Galton, who had been looking uneasy, smiled.

"Well, perhaps not in so many words," she said. "But he

hinted at it. And it came into my mind, like, that I'd have a bit of a joke on Galton, putting those two doctors' bones for him to see. He was too smart to be took in, Frank was. Dr Frost, too."

"So the hoax was really your idea, was it? I thought you said just now it wasn't."

"In a manner of speaking I suppose it was."

"I still don't understand how you came to think of it. Except that in Upfold none of you have believed that Mrs Wainwright went away at all, have you?"

She said this with deliberate sharpness and got the result she expected. Mrs Galton's face set into obstinacy, her eyes, fixed steadily on Mrs Frost, grew hard. She said, "It wasn't our place to have opinions of that nature, madam."

Mrs Frost decided to see Mrs Thompson at once before Mrs Galton could warn her, but when she reached the former's house she found she was out and remembered that she could probably be found at Mrs Graveney's. Mrs Frost was unwilling to pursue her there and went on out of the village, in the direction of the Cutfield's farm.

She was walking that morning as her husband had taken the car to London. The downs were misty in the late June sunshine, the hedgerows filled with wild roses. She felt inclined to turn from her present purpose and simply walk on until she reached the narrow lane that led to those rounded distant hills. She longed to climb away from the village which seemed now to lie under a dark cloud, a blight that clung to it and spoiled its image for her, for her husband, and surely for all those of its inhabitants who still harboured a secret as grim and soiled and ancient as the bones Harry had dug up.

But she kept to her main purpose. She was not a Scot for nothing. Tenacity, honesty of purpose and a sort of dour satisfaction in performing unpleasant tasks had served her many times before and they served her now. She had in her bag the farm account for milk, eggs and home-made butter. She knew she would find Mrs Cutfield to take the money.

The farmer's wife was pleased to see her. She liked Mrs Frost and was flattered by Dr Frost's interest in her young brother-in-law's medical career. She asked the doctor's wife to join her in a cup of synthetic coffee which she was preparing for herself, her domestic and her dairy staff. Afterwards, as the farmer's wife began to skim cream for her churn off wide pans of milk, Mrs Frost stayed to talk to her.

It was natural to begin again with the hoax. Jim Cutfield had been most annoyed; young Winter had been told off.

"George wanted to give him the sack, but I wouldn't let him. It was only a prank after all."

"Was it?"

Mrs Cutfield reddened.

"You mean now it turns out there were real bones? Well, I don't know. There are things—"

She broke off.

"Such as?" Mrs Frost asked. And as the other did not answer she went on, "There have been *things*, as you call them, about Mrs Wainwright ever since we came here. We're getting a bit fed up with it all."

"I don't blame you," said Mrs Cutfield, vigorously.

"Do *you* remember the night she disappeared?" Mrs Frost asked, deciding to cut any further caution in her approach.

"I remember it well."

Mrs Cutfield was smiling. Obviously she had a tale to tell that had been a success before and which she was pleased to present to the newcomer.

"There'd been this dog after our sheep. I don't mean Wainwright's dog. He'd got rid of it. This was later on. No one ever saw it and George was getting madder and madder. And no wonder with the poor things mauled—a shocking sight—and two dead. So he took his gun and not for the first time and went after it that night. Said he'd stay up till dawn if necessary but he'd get the brute if it was the last thing he did."

"And did he find it? Shoot it?" Mrs Frost asked.

"Of course not. Didn't even see it. Not a sight nor a sound. And nothing known of it from that day to this."

"You mean there was no further trouble with the sheep?"

"Nothing."

"But he didn't shoot it?"

"I told you. Didn't catch a glimpse of it."

"I was only thinking—" said Mrs Frost and stopped, appalled at her thought.

"Yes?"

"I was thinking of what they say in the village. About Mrs Wainwright being a witch and a were-wolf and this was the night she went and if Mr Cutfield had shot—"

She shivered. But Mrs Cutfield was laughing, aloud and heartily.

"That's a good one," she said. "I'll tell George that one. No. He didn't shoot anything. And when he came home—at dawn it was, too, and we heard later Mrs Wainwright had gone, I asked him, joking like, if he'd been with her, knowing well she'd been with Mr Farnham, you see. I asked George if he'd been with her and done away with her and you should have seen his face!" Mrs Cutfield was laughing again, her stout figure shaking all over with mirth. "I thought he'd blow up in my face. It was a scream, I can tell you."

"Yes," said Mrs Frost, trying to share in the amusement but finding it difficult after the fright she had given herself.

Dr Frost did not think the story at all funny, either. But it made a deep impression on him, because it reminded him of something that had happened shortly after their arrival at Upfold.

"D'you remember the first time we met Cutfield?" he asked.

"When we came home after our first tea party with Mrs Graveney and found him and his jeep at the gate?"

"Yes. And he offered to supply us with—"

"Milk and eggs and —" Mrs Frost stopped, remembering.

"And hens for the hen-run," finished Dr Frost. "So perhaps

he didn't want me to dig it up. Young Jim told me today at St Edmund's he was coming down next weekend. I think I'll wait and go along and tackle the pair of them."

Having rung up the farm on Saturday morning to ask if he might call, Dr Frost set off to walk there in the cool of the evening. Any time after eight, Mrs Cutfield had said.

The evening was fine, the sun still shining low on the horizon; a gentle air stirred the tops of the trees, but hardly penetrated to the lane; the swallows flew high; there were no clouds anywhere.

On such an evening it was difficult to believe that melodrama and mystery had ever visited this peaceful village, lying so sheltered, so cosily clustered about its ancient church. But in Dr Frost's mind the bones he had discovered still cried out, first for positive identification and then for the reason why they had lain where he found them. He hoped that in the next hour some progress would be made in both these directions.

On arriving at the farm his interest quickened. For not only the farmer and his brother were there waiting for him, but Pawley, whom he had so signally failed to impress only a few days before, was there too, looking both uncomfortable and aggressively defensive.

Mrs Cutfield had been with them until the doctor arrived, but after she had taken him into the room where they were and collected her work basket and mending, she went out, without making any excuse and left the four men to themselves.

There was a little pause after she had closed the door. Dr Frost had no intention of wasting time on small talk, whether or not it was designed to lead towards his purpose in being there. So he waited, quietly, as he had so often waited in his surgery, for the other side to begin, for truth to rush out into the silence, as it had usually done in those now distant times.

It was the farmer who began.

"My wife tells me your good lady's been asking her questions, doctor. About the night Mrs Wainwright went. So you'll have heard how I set out that night to find the rogue that was savaging my sheep."

"Yes. But you neither found nor saw a glimpse of it. And you were not home until dawn. And Mr Pawley was with you."

The butcher stirred a little in his chair but said nothing. Jim looked curious and interested. He did not seem to have heard of this expedition at all, or perhaps he had forgotten it.

"There was mist came up just after midnight," Cutfield went on, steadily. "A low mist, neck high in the lane. As we passed Mulberry Cottage we couldn't see the front door, nor the drive. Not clearly, you understand. But the bedroom windows at the front were in broad moonlight."

Pawley, who had become more and more restless as this careful description went forward, now burst into speech.

"What's the good of beating about the bush, George? Dr Frost don't want to hear about the weather. It's *her* he's inquiring after." He turned to face the doctor. "We found her," he said, in a sort of desperate eagerness. "We found her, lying in her bed—dead."

George nodded.

"That's the truth of it," he agreed.

"In her bed?" Dr Frost insisted.

"Yes, under the covers. Quite dead. Stiff. I reckoned she'd been dead three or four hours."

"How had she died?"

Cutfield and Pawley glanced at each other, then spoke at once.

"Took her own pills—"

"There wasn't a sign of any injury—"

They repeated their statements severally. Dr Frost said, "What pills? How d'you know that?"

Pawley explained.

"There was a bottle of pills in her handbag. What I mean, those long-shaped things—blue, these were—"

"You mean capsules?"

"That's right. In her handbag. It was on the dressing table, open. You could see the bottle just looking into the bag."

"We had a look at her," Cutfield said. "There wasn't a sign of violence on her at all."

"And then?"

"We buried her."

There was a long silence. Jim Cutfield was staring at his brother, horror in his face. Pawley had gone very pale. He took out his handkerchief and wiped his forehead and balding head.

"And when you did that, you drove a stake through her heart and cut off her head. Didn't you? *Didn't you?*" Dr Frost swept on without waiting for an answer. "You took her head and her clothes and her handbag and you burned them in Pawley's incinerator. Why?"

Pawley buried his face in his hands. Cutfield, less moved by recollection, nodded.

"That's about it," he said.

"Why not ring up the police and tell them you'd discovered a suicide? Or why not simply leave her for her husband to find next day?"

"He'd been good to me," Cutfield mumbled and told Dr Frost how Wainwright had helped him over the farm and how he'd wanted to spare the old man such a terrible shock.

"Was it kinder to bury her, leaving him in doubt? Leaving him to imagine she'd left him, perhaps alone, perhaps with someone he knew."

"We didn't think of it that way," Cutfield was plainly confused.

"She was a witch," Pawley said, hoarsely. "She had to be buried that way to stop her evil ways. If we'd left her she'd have been buried in the churchyard here. Sacrilege and no end to her haunting and her wickedness."

Dr Frost rose to his feet. He was filled with disgust and anger. Two grown men, not unintelligent like the Winter boy and his terrible old grandmother. The thought of their behaviour after their discovery that night sickened him.

"I shall not report what you have told me," he said. "But I shall have to tell Inspector Falk that you can give him some information about the bones I found. Obviously you will tell him the story you have told me."

"Which is the truth," said Cutfield, strongly.

"As God's my witness," said Pawley.

"But not the whole truth," said Dr Frost. "You have told me what you found in the bedroom at Mulberry Cottage. You have not told me why you went into the house at all. Inspector Falk will want to know that, won't he? Also, without the skull, how can we decide that there was no head injury? How can we be sure that on your night prowling you two didn't come across Mrs Wainwright and either attack her because you hated and feared her, or shot her in mistake for the dog you were gunning for? Inspector Falk will think of this, too, and demand an explanation. Won't he?"

The two older men seemed to be stunned. Jim half rose from his chair but his brother put out a hand to push him back.

"I'll handle this," he said, gruffly.

Dr Frost left the room and made his way from the farmhouse to the lane without meeting anyone on the way. He caught up Dick Winter at the first cross roads. The boy took off his cap as the former passed, less in acknowledgment than to scratch his rough mop of hair. His face was as vacant as ever. In-breeding and ill-bringing-up had done their work there, the doctor thought despondently. But he cheered up a little when he got home.

"Well, that's a nice big bit of news to get on with," his wife said, when she had heard the latest development. "Now you can sit back and let the police cope. You needn't worry your head over those bones any longer."

CHAPTER XI

In spite of his wife's admonition, Dr Frost continued to worry over the death of Celia Wainwright, for though Scotland Yard, informed of the confessions of Cutfield and Pawley, had taken up the case as one of potential suicide, if not murder, the investigators, as far as Upfold was concerned, appeared to have come to an end and this seemed to him very peculiar, to say the least of it.

He went to London again and saw Dr Wallace and as a consequence of this the latter paid a visit to Mulberry Cottage the following weekend.

"You see, Philip, we've got to make Marshall talk," Dr Frost said. "He knows more about Celia than he's willing to tell me. But with your backing we might get him to speak."

"Will you ask him to come here or go to see him at his own home?" Mrs Frost asked.

The three of them were sitting in the shade of the mulberry tree drinking coffee after lunch. Dr Wallace felt particularly peaceful and most unwilling to undertake any activity whatever on such an unusually fine sunny July afternoon.

"Here," he said, without hesitation and added, looking at Mrs Frost, "if Jeanie can face entertaining in this weather."

"I'll ask them both," Mrs Frost said. "Then I can latch on to Mrs Marshall, who's certain to offer to help me with the washing up and you and Harry can have a good go at Dr Marshall. Dinner today or lunch tomorrow?"

"I'll ring up and see," Dr Frost said.

Mrs Marshall, who answered the call, accepted the dinner invitation, pleased with the informality of being asked at such short notice. Dr Marshall, who had his suspicions of its object, since he recognised the name of Philip Wallace, raised a few feeble objections, but his wife overbore them. She liked Mrs Frost, with whom she had much in common.

Having laid in a good supply of food for Dr Wallace's visit Mrs Frost had no difficulty in rearranging her menus for the weekend. Her excellent lunch was followed by a superlative dinner, after which, as she had foreseen, she found herself alone with Mrs Marshall while the three men drifted out into the garden.

"Harry is showing them round his improvements, as he calls them," she said. "We'll give them plenty of time and take them out coffee when we've cleared up, shall we?"

Though the three doctors continued to move about the garden their conversation was not concerned with horticulture. Dr Marshall, anxious to keep the conversation away from the subject he feared to discuss, tried to talk about flowering shrubs, but Dr Wallace, moving firmly towards his intended objective, made this impossible. Halting near the toolshed he said, thoughtfully, "So *that* was the position of the famous hen-run?"

"Yes," said Dr Frost. "That was where they buried her, poor girl."

Dr Marshall was startled, as the other two meant him to be. He exclaimed aloud, checked himself and then burst out, "*Who* buried *whom?*"

"Cutfield and Pawley buried Celia Wainwright," Dr Wallace said, firmly. Dr Frost recited the tale as he had heard it.

Dr Marshall continued to look both upset and bewildered.

"Shall we go and sit down?" Dr Frost said, gently. "I thought you might have heard the gossip. I believe the whole village knows—have known, some of them—for years—perhaps from the start."

"Not this," Dr Marshall said. "Not the majority, I could swear. Suicide! Poor Celia. And she hoped to find happiness at last. Poor girl. Poor girl."

When they had all three sat down and Dr Marshall had lit a steadying cigarette, Dr Frost said, "Perhaps you would like to tell us now anything you know about Mrs Wainwright. You are certain to be asked by the police. I'm surprised they haven't been on to you already."

"Falk saw me about the bones," Dr Marshall said, defensively.

"I mean Scotland Yard."

"They've put Detective-Chief-Superintendent Mitchell in charge," Dr Wallace said. "The D.P.P. told me he's checking up on Wainwright for a start."

"She should never have married him!" Dr Marshall burst out, passionately. "A man of sixty-five, even if he did look no more than fifty. Everyone thought it was disgraceful, but they accused her of gold-digging all the same. It was not that at all. She married him to escape from her job and a man in it who would not leave her alone. She thought if she married Wainwright and lived in the country she might be able to lead a quiet life for a change."

"But it turned out just the opposite," Dr Frost suggested.

"It did. Most people were suspicious of Wainwright and disapproved of her. That is to say until Graveney O.K.'d him, because he knew his business position in London. The Singletons befriended her because Lady Singleton is one of the kindest and least snobbish people I have ever met."

"Jeanie would agree with that," said Dr Frost, warmly.

"This was before the village went round the bend over poor Celia," Dr Marshall continued. "They were a bit overcome by her looks. Not the sort they were used to—that very fair shining hair and delicate features—and so quiet with it all. But after the Thompson boy—well, then it boiled up. If ever there was mass hatred it was here—horrible!"

"Did she never go away on holiday—abroad or anything?" Dr Wallace asked.

"Not as far as I know. She had no relations in this country. Her mother was in Australia, living with her stepfather and the children of the second marriage. She told me she left there because she couldn't stand her home life. She'd given up writing to her mother and the mother never wrote to her."

"No wonder, then, there was so little fuss when she disappeared. Her isolation was greater than we imagined," Dr Frost said.

"It was almost complete. That was why, when she met—when she fell for someone—"

"Julian Farnham," supplied Dr Frost. "It's common knowledge. You're not giving anything away."

"I know I'm not. The point is she'd made up her mind to leave Wainwright."

"Ah!"

It was Dr Wallace who exclaimed and Marshall looked at him, nodding his head.

"The forensic pathologist at work," he said, with a faint professional smile. "Oh yes, you've guessed right. It needed her pregnancy to make up her mind for her."

"Julian?" asked Dr Frost, with a sigh.

"She thought so. He doesn't deny the possibility but has never been convinced. He was extremely shocked by her disappearance. It was he who told me she'd made up her mind to leave Wainwright."

"And go off with him?"

"He wanted her to ask for a divorce. She was against it for a long time. She told him Wainwright would never agree to divorce her and the only way was to go off together and force his hand."

"But Farnham was against that?" Dr Wallace suggested.

"How d'you know? Yes, he was when she told him that. He daren't risk a case for enticement and damages and that sort of thing. Without a divorce. He was younger than Celia—only just at the start of his writing career. Didn't want to give it up and perhaps have to go back to his old job to keep them both, if he was let in for large sums in litigation. Not to mention the child."

"So he stalled and she—Did her husband know she was pregnant?"

"She told me she hadn't told him, but he knew. She was only a bit over three months gone and they weren't sharing a bedroom—or a bed either, except very occasionally, by this time. She was frightened of him, especially when she realised that he knew about the child."

"The village accused her of witchcraft, but it looks more as if Wainwright had the powers of darkness," said Dr Frost, refilling his pipe.

"The poor girl seems to have had a particularly raw deal all round," Dr Wallace said.

The two wives now appeared, Mrs Frost carrying the coffee tray. After they had spent another half-hour in general conversation the midges drove them all indoors and soon after this a telephone call for Dr Marshall, transferred from his own number, sent him off on an urgent visit after dropping his wife at home and collecting his medical bag from the surgery.

Dr Wallace proposed a visit to Julian Farnham the next morning, so Dr Frost and he walked along the lane fairly soon after breakfast. The writer's house, however, was empty. At any rate there was no response to their ring and knock, so they walked on, climbed the nearest part of the downs and did not return to Mulberry Cottage until lunch time. Dr Wallace went back to London that evening.

Early in the week Mrs Frost met Mrs Graveney at a meeting of the Upfold and District Women's Institute. The latter made a point of sitting next to the doctor's wife and after the meeting was over cadged a lift home in the Frosts' car.

"Mine is in for an oil and grease," Mrs Graveney explained. "Miss Wilson brought me here but she's going off to Horsham directly and can't spare the time to take me back. So if you'd be an angel—"

"Of course," said Mrs Frost, good-naturedly, fully aware of Mrs Graveney's ulterior motive.

This emerged, without further subterfuge, when they arrived at the 'cloche-hat house' as the Frosts now called it.

"You must come in for a drink," Mrs Graveney said. "I

really insist. I want you to tell me all the latest developments."

Mrs Frost was not very willing to do this. The weekend revelations about Julian Farnham, formerly mere rumour and suspicion, had disturbed her greatly. Judy had been attracted to the man and he to her. She did not know if the friendship was still developing, but in any case she did not want her daughter to be involved with a man caught up in a perplexing mystery, all the more likely, because it had attracted no press notice hitherto, to burst into horrible publicity at any moment.

"I've heard such extraordinary rumours lately," Mrs Graveney began, "and since you and your husband began it all I'm sure you know the facts and can tell me which bits are pure fiction."

"I'm sure neither Harry nor I began anything," Mrs Frost protested, quite nettled by the idea that anyone should look upon her as an interfering busy-body. "It began ten years ago when Celia Wainwright's body was buried in our garden."

Mrs Graveney nodded eagerly.

"That's official, is it? All this talk about Cutfield and the butcher chopping her up—"

"So it's growing, is it?" Mrs Frost's voice was grim. "You'd better know the truth as far as I've heard it."

"That's just what I want," said Mrs Graveney, "to stop the nasty rumours."

And be right in the forefront of the news, Mrs Frost thought, but she went on with her account of the facts. When Mrs Graveney had heard it all and it did not, of course, include Dr Marshall's confidences about Celia's medical condition, she said, "Poor girl! Poor persecuted girl! So she committed suicide, did she? I always said Julian would let her down."

Mrs Frost winced. This might well be the truth of it. For Judy's sake she wanted to know more about the man.

"Tell me about Mr Farnham," she said. "It seems pretty certain Celia was having an affair with him. Was that widely known?"

"Of course. It was obvious to all of us who knew them both. We expected the balloon to go up any day."

"You mean Mr Wainwright would take steps to divorce her?"

"Yes. Or she would ask him for a divorce. I'm not sure she didn't. Wainwright was a very possessive sort of man. An odd type, we thought. Very cheery and charming on the surface— I think his big business success was built on that—but stone cold underneath."

She gave an artificial little shiver and laughed. Mrs Frost saw nothing to laugh at.

"What was Julian doing? Did he simply accept the fact that Celia might not get a divorce? Didn't he want to bring matters to a head, settle the affair one way or the other. Didn't he want to *marry* the girl?"

Mrs Graveney laughed again, this time in genuine amusement.

"My dear, he was scared stiff! He had practically no money and he got the idea Wainwright might sue him for enticement—don't they call it? No divorce—injunctions—damages —the lot! Poor boy, no wonder he let her down. But I don't suppose he thought for a moment she'd go and kill herself. No one would. She wasn't a neurotic type at all. Just very quiet and reserved. The village never understood her."

"They certainly didn't." Mrs Frost considered for a moment and went on. "Pawley apparently says he saw her blue capsules in her handbag. He burned the lot, the idiot, together with the clothes that were lying on the chair in the bedroom. She had a mild sleeping drug she was taking, but it wouldn't have killed her unless she took the lot. It looks as if she'd got hold of something far stronger or else—"

"Or else she was given it," Mrs Graveney suggested. "That's what you mean, isn't it?"

"One can't help wondering, especially if, as you say, she wasn't a suicidal type."

The two women looked at each other, Mrs Frost with a

123

growing fear for Judy in her heart, Mrs Graveney, always eager for stimulating news, flogging her memory.

"Mabel Snell!" she exclaimed. "You know who I mean?"

"The artist?"

"So-called. Terrible woman. Fell for Julian the moment he arrived. Green with jealousy when he got to know Celia. She takes drugs in a big way. I know that for a fact. I wouldn't be at all surprised if she didn't give Celia something."

"Are you suggesting she *murdered* Mrs Wainwright?"

Mrs Graveney, a little confused, came down from the height of fancy where she had been stumbling.

"No, no. Not *that*! I do hope there's no suggestion *of that* in the case. Celia might have told her she was desperate and Mabel, sorry for her, offered—well, *something*."

"I think we'd better not go on with that idea," Mrs Frost said, firmly, getting up to go. Mrs Graveney's goodbye to her was distinctly cool.

It is probable that neither Dr Frost nor his wife would have given Miss Snell a serious thought had it not been for her small one-man retrospective exhibition of paintings, in oil and tempera, held at the Public Library in Stourbridge. The oils were chiefly portraits, the tempera, still life. Of the former, no less than six depicted the same model. They had no difficulty in deciding, even without the catalogue, that this must be Celia Wainwright herself.

The paintings as a whole were derivative, mediocre, uninspiring. What the Frosts found immediately interesting and later totally absorbing, was the change and development in the treatment of Celia's beautiful person.

The earliest two pictures, painted, according to their dates, in the first six months after the Wainwrights' arrival in Upfold, were conventional, academic representations of the sitter. The obvious beauty of her features had been deliberately prettified by her pose, dress and surroundings until the results looked more like magazine covers than portraits. The third, nearly a year later, showed a marked change. Celia's beauty was still apparent but the face was now a mask, without life or expression. A gloomy, empty background added to the strangeness of the whole picture.

But it was the last three, painted in rapid succession during the two months before Celia's disappearance, that made the Frosts exclaim and hold their breath. These three pictures were grouped together, almost the last in the exhibition. No name was attributed to them, only the date of their production. It would have been difficult to identify them with the other three, at the far end of the room, but the Frosts knew whom they represented. Celia now appeared as a woman of haggard, unnatural beauty, a face full of malevolence, of barely controlled vicious hate, of brooding malignant intensity of purpose.

"Celia Wainwright in the role of the Upfold witch," said Dr Frost, grimly.

"As seen by her friend and well-wisher, Mabel Snell," said Mrs Frost, who shuddered as she spoke.

"Seen by the frustrated sub-conscious of Mabel Snell, I'm afraid," said Dr Frost, sadly. "Have I ever shown you some drawings a patient of mine, mental case, did of her husband?"

"Of course I saw them—several times."

"The first time she brought me one I felt like getting police protection for the poor chap."

"But she was certified before she did him any real damage, wasn't she?"

"Luckily, yes."

"It was Mrs Graveney," said Mrs Frost, thoughtfully, "who suggested Miss Snell may have had something to do with Celia's death. Handed her a lethal dose or rammed it down her neck."

"Or merely popped it into her pill bottle."

"She'd notice the difference. Her own were blue capsules."

"Mabel could have decanted a lethal dose into a blue capsule, at that."

Mrs Frost nodded.

"So could Julian or the Wainwright husband himself."

"Always provided they had access to a drug that could be crammed in a lethal dose into one or at most two capsules. Well, say three, if the stated dose was one to three."

"You'll have to ask Dr Marshall, won't you?"

But Marshall was only partly helpful. He had prescribed some powerful pills to Miss Snell for her persisting insomnia. He had given Wainwright a sedative drug to control his blood pressure. He was not Julian's doctor.

"I wish we'd never met Julian Farnham!" Mrs Frost exclaimed on hearing this.

"You're thinking of Judy, of course," said her husband, with a kind smile.

"What if I am! She fell in love with him at first sight. I know she did. He's a bad man, isn't he? Everything we hear—"

"We always hear the bad things about people first, don't we?" said Dr Frost, gently. "Come and see what I've bought."

Unsuspecting, Mrs Frost went into the study. Leaning against the doctor's desk was the last portrait of Celia, in all its outrageous spite.

"How *could* you!" she cried, deeply shocked.

"It's a curious psychological phenomenon," he explained. "Snell under the influence of village hysteria or her own emotional upheavals or both. Fascinating!"

"Obscene!"

"No. But possibly criminal. Libellous, I do believe."

"What did you really buy it for, Harry?"

"Oh, Jeanie, persistent woman! To bring here, of course. She never meant it to be recognised, far less sold. But they didn't know that at the Public Library."

CHAPTER XII

Inspector Falk took statements from Cutfield and Pawley with an ill-concealed sense of grievance. It was bad enough having old Dr Frost going over his head to his London medical pals and from that move beginning the interference of the Yard. Now the doctor had jumped the gun again with this precious pair of fools.

"That prehistoric stuff won't go down with the jury at the inquest, you know," he told Pawley in a sour voice. "Nor with the magistrates. How you can go on repeating it—Honestly!"

His contempt shone in his hard eyes. Pawley said nothing. His beliefs remained unshaken, bound as they were by undying grief for his child. None the less he was anxious. Cutfield looked extremely worried.

"Jury? Magistrates?" he asked, indignantly. "We didn't kill her. What've we done?"

"Concealed a death," the inspector answered, briskly. "For all I know, compounded a felony. It was your duty to inform the police when you found her. Or a doctor, first. Both, in the circumstances, if what you say is true."

"Of course it's true," protested Pawley, recovering.

"Very well, then. Now perhaps you'll tell me how you gained access to Mulberry Cottage, if Mrs Wainwright was already dead, lying in an upstairs room."

"We used a shed roof to get in by the bathroom window, which was open."

"Breaking and entering, eh? No answer to the bell or knock? Or didn't you try?"

There was silence.

"Didn't you try?" Falk repeated. "You come to a house where you know a young woman is alone, her husband being away on business. You get there a bit after midnight, according to your statement. You give no reason for approaching the house."

"We were looking for that dog," Cutfield said, sulkily.

"In Mulberry Cottage? In the garden? Or did you think Mrs Wainwright was hiding it in the house? No, Mr Pawley!" He held up his hand as he saw Pawley's mouth twitch. "You can't sell me that fairy tale. I advise you again you'd best forget it, unless you want to land yourself in the nuthouse. Did you expect to find the dog at Mulberry Cottage, Mr Cutfield?"

"No."

"Then why did you go up to the house? Why ring and knock?"

"We did neither."

"I thought as much. Breaking and entering, eh?"

Cutfield was exasperated.

"If you like," he said, impatiently. "But not as you think."

"How d'you know what I think?"

"Not as burglars. You can pass that up for a start."

As Falk made no response the farmer went on in a louder voice, "We've told you what we told Dr Frost. If what we did was illegal—"

"You know bloody well it was illegal!"

Cutfield was suddenly furious.

"Then act on that anyway you damn well like. We're not saying another word. You can do your own dirty work."

Pawley grunted agreement. Falk knew he would not get anything further from either of them. So he told them they could go, but must not leave the district as they would be wanted again at any time.

"Leave the district!" Pawley muttered, as they walked towards Cutfield's jeep. "Where d'you think we get our money?"

Cutfield did not answer. He and his friend had decided not to mention Julian and had stuck to it even when they realised the seriousness of their actions. It would only make their behaviour look worse. But it was worrying—very worrying indeed.

After this trying interview Inspector Falk felt particularly depressed, until a trunk call for him from London produced Dr Wallace on the line.

"I thought you ought to know," the pathologist was saying. "Dr Marshall prescribed a very mild drug for Mrs Wainwright but he had three patients at Upfold on something stronger. Mrs Wainwright was allowed up to four of her things at night, one or two during the day. Four of the stronger ones would be lethal."

"So?" asked the inspector, guardedly.

"So the three other patients were her husband, Miss Snell and an old Mrs Cowley. I got this last from Dr Marshall yesterday. He'd just repeated her prescription."

"Oh no!" groaned Falk. Wainwright he had already considered. Also Miss Snell, who if rumour was correct had a crush on Julian Farnham. But Mrs Cowley, who'd been the poison tongue all through! It was too much, but he had to accept it.

"Thanks a lot," he said. "That gives me another fresh lead. I'll get on to it at once."

"I should," Dr Wallace advised him. "Before any of them know what your present line is. And before the Yard arrives in Upfold. I don't know if your Chief Constable has told you, but you're getting Detective-Chief-Superintendent Mitchell, very keen, very experienced. It's quite irregular for me to ring you at all, but I know my friend Dr Frost."

"Thank you, sir," said Falk, more formally. "I understand. I have been informed. I hope I'll have something useful for the Super when he comes."

Dr Wallace said, "You realise the press will be on to this now? Surprising they haven't been, before."

"They got the hoax angle all right," Falk told him. "We let them play that as a silly sort of practical joke. We couldn't very well prosecute. Mrs Thompson and Dick Winter weren't guilty of breaking and entering—they were employed by Dr Marshall and Mr Cutfield. They had legitimate access to the surgery and the farm. Neither of the half skeletons was locked up. They were just in boxes in cupboards."

Dr Wallace rang off. He was no longer interested in the Upfold case. The identity of the bones was now certain, the cause of death could never be proved.

Superintendent Mitchell arrived in Upfold with a detective-sergeant the same day, before Inspector Falk had had time to see Miss Snell or Mrs Cowley. After hearing Falk's account of his conversation with Dr Wallace, Mitchell decided to begin with the old woman. Falk went with him. The sergeant drove the Yard car.

They found her alone in the Winters' house, except for a girl of about twelve, who let them in and after an argument, during which she blocked the narrow front passage with her short stout person, agreed to stand aside, though she raised her voice in shrill warning as the three men went past her.

Consequently they found old Mrs Cowley in a state of considerable agitation, half risen from her chair and gasping. When Mitchell explained who they were she sank back, still breathing heavily, with a hand pressed to the front of her greasy blouse.

"The child who let us in didn't get what we wanted," Falk said, irritably. "Isn't that Maisie Winter? I thought she went to a special school."

"They've got the mumps at 'er school," Mrs Cowley said. "My daughter kept 'er at 'ome. She's bad enough as it is, without the mumps."

"Mild M.D.," Falk said aside to Superintendent Mitchell.

" 'Andicapped," Mrs Cowley corrected, fiercely. "That's wot they calls 'er. 'Andicapped."

"I'll say," Falk answered, unrepentant.

Mitchell intervened. This was definitely not getting the old woman into the right frame of mind for his questions. He said, in a friendly voice, "I'm from London, Mrs Cowley. I

130

wanted to see you about Mrs Celia Wainwright, who died in Upfold ten years ago."

Mrs Cowley showed no signs of shock, but her old eyes took on a look of cunning that gave the superintendent a most unpleasant feeling.

"So that's wot they thinks now, is it?" she remarked. "Taken their time over it, I must say."

"I'm not going to discuss her death with you," the superintendent went on. "I think you know as much about it as anyone. I shall take that for granted. What I want from you is why you chose to slander the poor young woman while she was alive."

"And wot d'yer mean by that?" asked Mrs Cowley with a truculent note in her grating voice.

"You spread a ridiculous, but vicious rumour about her. Called her a witch or some such wicked nonsense."

"It warn't no nonsense. She 'ad the power. I seed it meself."

Both Mitchell and Falk shook their heads impatiently. The sergeant merely looked bored.

"That's nonsense, too. I don't believe you really thought any such thing."

"Call me a liar, do you?" Mrs Cowley stared at them with hatred. "Coming in 'ere, abusing a poor old woman that can't stop yer. Bullies, the pair on yer. Coppers!"

She spat on the floor between their feet. If she had been strong enough she would have spat in their faces, Mitchell thought. A venomous old snake, with the will to strike, but no longer the power.

"What put such an idea into your head?" Mitchell persisted. "Or do you make a habit of going about calling people witches?"

Mrs Cowley was beginning to lose control of herself. She beat on the arm of her chair, her thin old legs shot out at the two officers near her in a paroxysm of fury. Her voice rose to a screech in which fear was now mixed with anger.

"Get out of 'ere!" she cried. "She were a witch, I knowed it and others better placed than me. I guessed it and 'e said so. 'E come 'ere 'isself and said so."

"Who came here and said so?" Mitchell asked quickly. The sergeant, who had held his pencil poised during most of the conversation, now wrote rapidly.

"Oo but 'isself?" Mrs Cowley answered, still raging. "Oh, she led 'im a dance and no mistake. Going with men every middle week. Thought 'e never knew, but 'e warn't no fool. Come to me and told me, plain. 'She be a witch, Mrs Cowley.' 'E never said a truer word."

"You are talking about Mr Wainwright, aren't you?" Mitchell said. His thoughts were running fast. A credulous old woman with a reputation for superstitious practices. A revengeful old man, using words that could mean simply that his wife was a very attractive woman, eager to injure her without himself taking any irrevocable steps. Or perhaps as a preliminary—He repeated his question.

But Mrs Cowley was staring beyond him at the door, was sinking down in her chair, fumbling in the pocket of her skirt for a filthy handkerchief that she pulled out to wipe away the line of froth that had gathered at the corners of her mouth. Both officers wheeled round. Mrs Winter, very pale, very calm, was standing in the doorway.

"Good morning, Mrs Winter," said Falk, uneasily. "We were just asking Mrs Cowley one or two questions about Mrs Wainwright."

"Taking advantage of poor Maisie to force your way into the 'ouse," said Mrs Winter, without heat, stating a fact.

"Force had nothing to do with it," Mitchell said. "We asked to come in and we were allowed to come in."

"I can't contradict you, seeing I wasn't 'ere to witness it," Mrs Winter answered and went up to her mother's chair. "'Ave they been bullying you, Gran?" she asked.

Mrs Cowley, who had recovered, shook her head. Mrs Winter asked her a few more questions. Mrs Cowley shook her head several times and shut her eyes.

"You've wore 'er out, at any rate," Mrs Winter said. "So per'aps you'll be kind enough to take yerselves off before you do 'er a serious injury."

Mitchell disregarded this. He looked sternly at Mrs Winter and said, "Was Mr Wainwright in the habit of coming to this house often?"

That shook her.

"Coming 'ere?"

"Your mother says he told her his wife was a witch. She spoke as if he often came to see her."

"Mother's over ninety, as Mr Falk knows, if you don't. You can't take what she says for gospel."

"'E told me," Mrs Cowley grunted, opening her eyes.

"You shut up!" said Mrs Winter, fiercely, showing emotion for the first time. She turned to the three men. "She's worse nor a child and that's a fact. If you want to know, Mr Wainwright called in once or twice to pay 'is laundry bill or get me to do a bit of extra pressing for 'im."

"Thank you."

With a glance at Falk and the sergeant Mitchell moved to the door. Mrs Winter watched them from her doorstep as they got into the police car and drove away. She watched them until they were out of sight. Then she went back to Mrs Cowley. But the old woman's eyes were closed again and she seemed to have fallen asleep. Mrs Winter spread her ironing cloth on the table.

Mitchell drove to Miss Snell's studio cottage. The artist was at work on a flower composition, but she laid aside her palette and brushes and welcomed the police officers politely, offering them drinks, which they refused. She would say very little about Mrs Wainwright until Mitchell began to talk about Julian Farnham.

"She nearly ruined him," Miss Snell said. "He was infatuated. Of course he was very young at the time. Quite three years younger than she was."

"You knew him well?"

"*Very* well." Miss Snell flushed a little. "You see we were the only artists in this place."

"I didn't know he painted."

"He doesn't. He writes. I used the word artist in the wider sense. The art of letters. He has—he had—a great talent."

"I see." Mitchell was determined not to be led astray into a discussion of art, that curious aberration of a minority of citizens.

"You were on—er—confidential terms? " he asked.

"What d'you mean by that? I wasn't his mistress," Miss Snell said, deliberately bohemian.

"But you think Mrs Wainwright was?" Mitchell said calmly, determined not to let Miss Snell impress him in any way.

"I know she was."

"He told you so?"

"Yes. He was at his wits' end. Couldn't afford to marry her—"

"I've heard all this."

"Very well. Then why ask me?"

Mitchell cursed himself for clumsiness. Falk, seeing the Yard put out, took up the thread.

"Simply because we know he valued your friendship, Miss Snell, and—"

"He values no one's friendship!" she burst out, violently. "He sucks you dry, he takes what he wants, only what he wants, he gives nothing—"

"That was how he treated you and that was how he treated Mrs Wainwright?"

"He treated her as she deserved. He must have made his meaning very plain for her to go straight home from him and kill herself."

"Was she at his house that night, then?"

"She was."

"D'you know that for a fact?"

"I do."

"How?"

Miss Snell seemed to be overcome by her recollections of the event.

"I saw her go in. He'd lied to me. He told me he was going to London that evening and did not know when he'd be back."

"When did he tell you this?"

"That same afternoon. He came here to my house to say good-bye. But he didn't go that night. He didn't go till the early hours of next morning."

"Were you watching him, Miss Snell?"

She nodded her head, with no shame, only a kind of desperate dignity.

"I didn't believe he would break it off. So when I saw her car go past up the road just after four, I went along and it was parked at his house. I went past three times that evening, that night. It was still there at midnight."

Superintendent Mitchell did some rapid sums in his head. Then, turning to Miss Snell, he said, "Are you prepared to make a statement on these lines? Do you realise what you have said?"

She looked bewildered.

"Mrs Wainwright's body was found in her own house at about two in the morning. She had been dead for over three hours, probably. If what you say is true—"

"Julian must have killed her!" Miss Snell's face was white. She cried out, furiously, "There was no limit to her wickedness! No end!"

"We are speaking of her death," Mitchell reminded her. "I repeat, are you prepared to make this statement on oath?"

"It's the truth," said Miss Snell.

The three officers drove back to Stourfield, not altogether satisfied with their work.

"If we knew what killed her, we'd have something to build on," Mitchell said.

Falk agreed.

"Dr Wallace thinks it may have been a drug substituted for her own stuff. Dr Marshall provided a possible one to Miss Snell and to Mrs Cowley. Wainwright had some sedative stuff, but not strong enough for a practical substitution."

"Could Farnham possibly have got some from Snell?"

"Presumably. Or he could have had something of his own. He isn't on Dr Marshall's list, nor any doctor's around here. May have a London doctor."

"Yes. What about Cowley?"

"I suppose Wainwright could have got at hers. I don't believe for a moment he went round to the laundress to pay his bill. A man of that type and standing wouldn't have his clothes pressed by Mrs Winter, even if Mulberry Cottage sheets went to her. No, if he visited the Cowley set-up it was in order to suggest a witch hunt to a very receptive old lady."

"That's a nasty thought," said Falk.

"The whole thing's a nasty business," Mitchell answered. "The press will go to town on it after the inquest."

"When's that to be?"

"Not for another week, at least. I want to go into old Wainwright's alibi for the night in question. We don't seem to know much about him, at all. I propose to get him up to town, if he'll play, and really go over him."

"It'll be a funny sort of inquest with a couple of bones only and a few very tall tales. I suppose Cutfield and Pawley will get run in for concealing a death, won't they?"

"I sincerely hope so."

"And Farnham as well? If Snell's tale is true. We'll have to see Farnham. Will you do that?"

"Yes, sir." Falk was not mollified by this sop. "We might have something more for him than concealing, don't you think?"

He spoke reluctantly. He rather hoped not. The case was out of his hands now so he had lost any incentive he had ever had, which was not much.

Mitchell and the sergeant went back to London. The

Superintendent found that Wainwright had most certainly been in town for the whole of the time covered by Celia's death and disposal. He had not left the city at all. As for his past, he had been born and brought up in England but had spent twenty years from the age of thirty-five in Canada, where he had founded the business, a branch of which he later brought to London. He had married Celia when he was sixty-five. He had retired from business soon after her death, when he was sixty-seven and had gone out again to Canada immediately. He had returned finally three years later, bringing his present wife with him. He was now seventy-five, living in Cornwall, at Trethuan, not far from Helston.

A blameless history? A too blameless history? Superintendent Mitchell searched in vain for flaws. Of course there was a lot to check, both in England and Canada. But the outline was plausible. Wainwright was not the only old man, vigorous for his age, who had married a young woman and been deceived by her. Nor was he the only old man who had put up with the horns for fear of public ridicule and humiliation in the divorce court. But Mrs Cowley had been too angry to lie and Mrs Winter too sly to be believed. And if the old man had encouraged the old woman to spread such a crudely filthy rumour what sort of old man did that make Mr Wainwright? Capable of anything, Mitchell was inclined to think.

CHAPTER XIII

During this time Judy had gone about her work as the hospital with a feeling of acute loss and desolation, though she told herself this was out of all proportion to her very transient acquaintance with Julian. She even suffered that definite physical ache in the chest inseparable from deep emotion and

137

which has produced so much poetical reference to the heart over the centuries. She was aware of her state, she resented it, she cherished it. She was a very normal girl very deeply in love.

Her surprise and joy, almost amounting to ecstasy, were therefore quite natural when Julian appeared suddenly one evening on her doorstep, himself distraught, urgently pleading for help and compassion. Fortunately the girl with whom she shared the flat was out for the evening, so Judy was able to welcome him in, provide him with a chair and a drink and encourage him to talk.

"I've got to tell you," he said, but got no further, only repeated the same phrase several times, in tones that became more and more desperate.

"Something about Mrs Wainwright?" asked Judy, fear keeping her from him, love urging her to take him in her arms to comfort him.

He nodded.

"What else? My God, what else has been nagging at me ever since your father dug up—"

He stopped, shivering so violently that he had to put down his glass on the floor beside him and clasp his hands together to stop their shaking.

"Tell me what happened that night! Whatever it was I don't believe you could help it!" Judy said, passionately. Even if he'd killed her it couldn't be his fault, she thought wildly, prepared to defend him against all laws, all the world.

Julian forced a bitter smile.

"I certainly couldn't help what happened," he said, slowly, "seeing I was asleep at the time."

Judy felt herself blushing and put her hands to her face to hide it.

"I woke up," Julian went on, grinding out the facts in a harsh voice. "I woke up and found her dead beside me. Dead—looking as if she was only asleep—but dead." He stared at Judy. "Can you believe that? No one else will."

"Of course I believe you," she said, gently. "That's what

you meant when you told me—how long ago it seems—
that she was capable of anything. Wasn't it?"

He stumbled across to her where she sat and for a long time
clung to her, seeking and finding the understanding he had
longed for in all the years since that terrible night. Presently
the whole story came out, stumblingly at first, then with
less hesitation, his storyteller's practised mind supplying a
continuous thread of illuminating detail.

In essence it was a simple tale. They had met in the normal
social exchange of visits. Celia was alone during the middle of
each week. His work was subject only to his own discipline.
He had no regular hours and at this time he was feeling his
way with great diffidence through his second novel, anxious
not to produce something similar and less fresh than the first,
but a real step forward in his development.

The friendship ripened, the book withered. Before long he
had abandoned work almost entirely, only goaded from time
to time by Mabel Snell and by an anxious publisher, who had
been agreeably surprised by his initial success, but had not
expected him to dry up so soon.

It was not long before thoughts of the future, in every
direction, began to torment him, distracting him further from
his feeble attempts to write and souring his passion for Celia.
"Didn't she realise what she was doing?" Judy asked,
indignantly.

"Oh, yes. It grieved her very much. She often said she
brought nothing but trouble to everyone."

"Couldn't she have—well, gone away or something?"

Julian shook his head.

"She was lovely—the most beautiful woman I have ever
seen—and quite empty, if you know what I mean. Not stupid
—far from it—not uneducated—quite a lot of ideas—but no
will, no initiative of any kind. You could do anything you liked
with her—except leave her."

"That was the power they all talk about."

"I suppose so."

"Tell me the rest of it. When you found her dead, what did you do?"

He described how he had first thought of getting Dr Marshall. Then he had recoiled from this. She was pregnant, probably with his own child, which was dead as well. He could not face an inquest at which all these facts would be displayed. He had meant to take her to London that night and force Wainwright to divorce her. They had planned to start very late; about two in the morning. So in order to get a reasonable amount of rest, particularly for her, they had had an early supper and gone to bed soon after, about seven. He had set his alarm clock for midnight. He had tried to wake her—

"She really meant to go with you?" Judy asked.

"Oh yes," Julian said.

She had agreed to his plan, as usual, but had brought nothing to his house in the way of luggage.

"Did she say why not?"

"She said everything she had was provided by Wainwright and she would not take it away when she left him."

"But she must have had clothes of her own when she married him. And other things."

"It was two years after."

"Some things last much longer than two years."

"Well, anyway that was what she said and I accepted it." His voice was impatient.

"I only meant perhaps she didn't really want to go—didn't mean to go."

He hid his face against her neck for a few moments, then lifted it again and said, "I thought of that. It has tortured me ever since. That she was so desperate between wanting to go and not wanting to, that she killed herself, there in my bed, after we'd loved each other for the last time."

Judy felt tears begin to roll down her cheeks, tears of sorrow for his pain, of grief for the waste of his life over ten years, tears of helplessness in her own predicament. Tears perhaps too for Celia and the lost child.

"I wasn't capable that night of any straight thinking," Julian went on, presently. "I only knew that whether it was an accident or deliberate, she mustn't be found in my house. So I took her home in her own car and put her in her own bed. I left the car in their garage. I left her clothes and her handbag with her bottle of capsules in it on her dressing table. I went back, took my suitcase, which I'd packed earlier that day, I mean the day before—it was two in the morning by now—and drove up to London alone. I'd borrowed a flat from some friends who were on holiday. They knew I meant to bring Celia, but afterwards they didn't mention this. Only said I'd come to their flat to stay."

"It must have been terrible for you when nothing happened."

"I nearly went out of my mind. Shock from her death and then not knowing when she'd be discovered and then nothing at all happening, going on and on—"

"My poor darling!" Judy sobbed, overcome by her feelings and in her turn burying her distress in a receptive shoulder.

Julian turned her face up to his.

"You know why I came here today to tell you all this?"

"Daddy rang me yesterday about Cutfield and Pawley."

"Yes. You see what that means, don't you?"

She caught her breath.

"They saw you take Celia into Mulberry Cottage! They must have. That's why they went in themselves."

"Yes. So the police will know what I did."

"Daddy said nothing about you. Perhaps they haven't told the police that bit."

"Perhaps not. But *I* shall have to tell them—the police, I mean. Shan't I?"

"Because they may suspect Cutfield and Pawley of killing her?"

"Because I can't keep it to myself now. We've got to clear the whole truth out of the way or this thing'll get between you and me again as it has done the last two weeks. And I can't stand that. I love you, Judy. You love me, don't you?"

"You know I do."

They kissed gravely in the shadow of Celia's fate and then hungrily, passionately, with all the strength of two ardent, long unfulfilled natures.

Presently Julian took his arms away and said, "Tomorrow's Friday. Do you have to work?"

"I think I could get leave."

"I want you to be at Mulberry Cottage when I see the cops at Stourfield. I think my statement will push on the inquest."

"Daddy said it might be on Monday. I shan't be able to stay on after Sunday."

"No. I'd rather you weren't there when I go into the witness box. The Stourfield coroner is a straight-laced old lawyer. He'll probably shop me for murder."

"Won't there be a jury?"

"I hope so. They're having it in Stourfield because an Up-fold jury would find suicide of malice aforethought, against any evidence that might be brought, and would acquit the lot of us."

His hard voice as he spoke and the callous words he used sent a sharp twinge of misgiving through Judy, but his eyes as he looked at her were soft and his hands, drawing her back into his arms, were gentle.

They drove down to Upfold together. Julian would not leave his car when they arrived at Mulberry Cottage, but drove away at once to his own house after handing Judy her suit-case. She went in to greet her parents, determined to tell them nothing about his revelations.

But she found her father anxious to discuss the case in the light of some further facts he had been given by Miss Snell. His plan, in buying the artist's picture of Celia had succeeded beyond his expectations. Miss Snell had arrived at the cottage on the morning after the exhibition closed, angry, frightened, thoroughly embarrassed, but in some strange way proud, too, even pleased.

"I find Upfold so entirely unresponsive to my work," she

declared. "It's a great joy to be appreciated for once."

It was Dr Frost's turn to be embarrassed.

"I don't want you to misunderstand me," he said. "The quality of the painting I am not able to judge, though it seems to be fully competent—"

"Competent!" groaned Miss Snell.

"The subject is recognisable—just. But the interpretation is a travesty—a libel—if you can have such a thing in a painting."

"D'you mean a caricature?" she demanded. "Because I had no humorous intention, I assure you."

"Certainly not. I mean a libel, in the sense of an attempt to injure a person by imputing evil to them."

"She *was* evil. I painted her as I saw her."

"I think not. You painted her as you had been brought to understand the village saw her. I don't believe for a moment this was your own true view of her."

"Why should I do that?" Miss Snell was indignant. Her voice rose, shrilly. "Why should I paint what I knew to be a lie?"

She swept back her long unbrushed hair from her forehead. She swung away from the doctor who was standing near the painting, turning her back upon both.

"Because you were jealous of her association with Julian Farnham. You were in love with him."

"How dare you!"

Miss Snell flung round again, red with anger. Tears sprang to her eyes. She fumbled for a handkerchief, trying to think of something to say that would annihilate this old man with his obscene curiosity. But no words came, only a harsh sob, followed by another and another, until Miss Snell collapsed on a chair, laid her head on Dr Frost's writing desk and wept her heart out for the first time in many years.

He waited patiently for her to recover. When at last she lifted her head, he said, very gently, "Can I get you a glass of water?"

Miss Snell nodded. She was dabbing her swollen eyes and

nose; a lamentable sight, poor child, thought Dr Frost, going out of the room. No one has ever loved her. But then she was, in nearly every way, so very unlovable.

"You've put something in it," Miss Snell said, choking a little as she gulped the bitter lemon drink the doctor had brought her.

"Only a little gin," he answered. "You need it."

She looked at him. She was empty now of all emotion and able to see, for once, something of the world about her and the people in it.

"You must have been a very good doctor," she said.

"Have been?" He smiled ruefully.

"Still are." She pulled at her unbecoming dress, which did nothing to improve its appearance. She drank the rest of her gin greedily. Then she said, continuing the conversation from the point where she had broken down, "Yes, I was jealous."

To justify herself a little she gave him an account of her activities on the night of Celia's disappearance, ending up by repeating, "I was beside myself with jealousy. I think that's over, now."

"Washed out by your tears," said Dr Frost. Seeing her lip begin to tremble he added, "As it should be. As all grief should be resolved."

"Yes. I see I've been cruel and unjust. Celia never looked like that—outwardly, I mean. I didn't know her well. She didn't like me and she knew she'd cut me out with Julian. But I'll tell you one thing you may not know. She was afraid of John—her husband. When she was upset over the Thompson boy she said to me once 'I never wanted him to fall in love with me. I did my best to put him off. I swear I did. It was John who encouraged him.'"

"She said that! In those words?"

"As near as I can remember. And then she begged me not to repeat it. She was afraid of him all right."

"From what you knew of her, did you put that down to imagination—nerves—mental instability?"

144

"Not for a moment. Celia was perfectly normal. Very quiet, very reserved, rather stupid, I think—and perfectly lovely."

"But in every way normal?"

"Quite normal."

Miss Snell, apparently recovered, got to her feet. She tried to apologise for making a scene, but gave it up. She went close to her picture and said, without turning her head, "Will you burn this, please? I'll give you back the price you paid for it."

"But then you'd have to give the dealer his commission, wouldn't you?"

"I'll do that. A penance."

"No," said Dr Frost. "I won't burn it. I think from the point of view of art it may be the best thing you've ever done. I shall try to sell it to an art gallery. It's too—well, too repellent—to hang up in a private house, don't you think?"

Miss Snell laughed, a genuine hearty professional laugh.

"Repellent?" she said. "It's cheesecake compared with some modern artists' things that go to private buyers for their own collections. Let me know where it goes, won't you?"

Dr Frost assured her that he would do so. In the meantime he turned Celia Wainwright with her witch face to the wall until the full story of her fate should be known.

So Judy, hearing the tale of this encounter, could not refrain from giving her father Julian's version.

"It may be true," he said, gravely. "I hope for your sake it is. I only trust he has not kept anything back."

"What d'you mean?"

But Dr Frost would not tell her.

The inquest took place on the following Monday. The evidence was sparse. It consisted of statements by Julian, Cutfield and Pawley, describing the discovery of the death, the moving of the body from Julian's house to Mulberry Cottage, the viewing and subsequent disposal of the corpse.

Mrs Thompson gave evidence of not being able to get into the cottage later that morning. Mr Wainwright, a tall upright old man with a steady eye and a firm tread as he crossed the court to the witness box, spoke of finding the house empty, a few of his wife's clothes and one handbag missing, the rest in place. He said he had not known of her affair with Julian, nor of her pregnancy. He was asked what steps he had taken to find her. His answers were reasonable. He was asked if he thought she intended to leave him that night. He said he would have expected her to take her more valuable possessions with her if that had been so. He was asked if he thought she had committed suicide. He said he had always felt it was on the cards she might have done so. She was unstable. He thought now that she must have done it.

The coroner found the witness difficult to handle and got rid of him as soon as he could. Dr Frost then described his own discovery. Dr Wallace followed with medical evidence relating to the material he had examined. Dr Marshall gave further medical evidence.

The public showed every sign of enjoyment. This inquest provided it with more delicious horror than it had been given for a long time. The press scribbled furiously and raced for telephones afterwards. The coroner gave a lecture on concealing evidence and a short exhortation on casting out superstition. The jury found the remains were those of Celia Wainwright, that there was insufficient evidence to give the cause of death, but that it had been brought about deliberately by some person or persons unknown. In other words, the verdict was one of murder.

CHAPTER XIV

Judy heard on Monday evening, from her father, the result of the inquest. She received the news with great foreboding, but not very much surprise. Too many people had hated Celia, or feared her. There was no real evidence of a suicidal tendency.

There were several people who might have poisoned her, hoping to simulate suicide. Julian, in particular. For any man, finding his lover dead beside him, to take such highly questionable, such cunningly efficient action instead of immediately calling for aid, was to condemn him in most British minds, so sentimental, so puritan. The situation, Judy saw at once, was inevitable and highly dangerous.

But on Tuesday a further complication arose to try her further. A letter from Julian, in a small parcel, arrived by the second post after she had gone to work. She did not get it until she came back from the hospital. It had been sent on Monday morning before the inquest opened. She wondered at first why he had written the letter, when they had said everything that could be said to one another, sitting on the cliffs above the sea at Cuckmere Haven. But when she opened the small packet round which the letter was folded, his object was made clear.

Inside there was a match box and in the box, lying in cotton-wool, there were two blue capsules. Looking at them Judy saw that it was the capsule itself that was blue in each case. The contents of each seemed to be a white substance.

She read the letter and then sat looking at the matchbox, trying to put down not only an added fear but a new doubt of Julian himself.

I found these capsules, he wrote, when I came back from Mulberry Cottage after leaving Celia there. I put them in this empty matchbox and took them to London with me. I suppose I ought to have given them to the police at Stourfield, but I'm sure they are trying to build a case against me and they could have used the fact of my possessing them to add to their score. The jury in the coroner's court would certainly name me on the strength of it. I swear I found them on the carpet near the bed table where Celia had put the bottle with the rest. She must have spilled some when she took her dose, whatever that was. You believe me, don't you? Don't you, my darling?

147

Judy forced herself to say in her mind, "Of course I do", but she knew the doubt was there, too. She read on.

If at the inquest the verdict is an open one, you know, mis-adventure, accident or suicide, impossible to say which, then burn these and we'll forget about them. But if it goes against me, personally, or even if it is brought in murder by person or persons unknown, then take them to Dr Wallace. It may help me in that case, if the stuff in them is something I could not have got hold of.

This offered some definite hope, Judy decided. She was ashamed of her gnawing doubts. In any case, doubt or not, she still loved Julian with all her heart and an opportunity to help him gave her exquisite pleasure. She rang up Dr Wallace at his home address and took the capsules to him the following morning. He insisted upon reading Julian's covering letter, after which he advised her to leave it to him. Superintendent Mitchell would have to be told about it and sent a report on the capsules. It could only help Julian to be perfectly frank with the police.

"I know all that," Judy said, impatiently, "but he's in danger. He must be."

"Not more so than several others, I think."

The days went by, no report came to Judy from Dr Wallace. She tried to ring him up on Thursday, when she was told by an assistant at the laboratory that the investigations were not complete. On Friday she tried again. This time a woman secretary explained that Dr Wallace was not available and hung up. On Saturday Judy went home for the weekend.

Julian, she knew, was not in Upfold. He had gone to see his parents in Reading. They had never approved of his career as a writer and were now appalled by the publicity surrounding him. He had gone to reassure them.

Judy had decided not to hold out on her parents any longer. It was not fair to them nor to herself and still less to Julian.

"You aren't definitely engaged to him, are you?" Mrs Frost almost wailed.

"Well, no. We haven't actually discussed getting married. There've been too many other things—"

"He's quite obviously not the marrying sort," Mrs Frost said, tartly.

"If you think that, we'd better stop talking about him," Judy answered, making for the door.

But Dr Frost stopped her.

"Come back and sit down," he said. "And Jeannie, do try to stick to the real point of all this. If Julian's story is true—all of it—he's had an undeservedly hard time for years. It's not surprising he hasn't married with all this hanging over his head."

"He didn't know what had happened to her body. He thought Wainwright must've taken it away."

"Why didn't he make inquiries, then?" Mrs Frost demanded.

"He couldn't, without giving himself away."

"Nor could Wainwright," said Dr Frost, thoughtfully. "Whatever part he had in this. Nor could any of them."

"So?"

"So we must wait for the result of the analysis."

Dr Frost looked at his wife and daughter. Their latent antagonism worried him, as always, knowing as he did that they were really very fond of each other.

"Of course Julian can't have murdered the woman," Mrs Frost said. "I'm fully prepared to believe him there. Personally I think if her capsules were tampered with, it must have been Miss Snell."

"I can't agree with you," said the doctor. "Old Mrs Cowley had the same sort and Mrs Thompson was in and out of the house."

"I don't care which of them did it," Judy said, fiercely, "if only we can find out and get rid of this threat to Julian."

"I'll see if I can stir up Philip," Dr Frost said.

Mrs Frost got up and left the room. She loved her daughter,

she wanted her to be happily married, she saw no possible chance of it with Julian. So she went upstairs to her own room and wrote a long explanatory letter to her elder son who had never given her any qualms and had supplied her with a charming daughter-in-law and two delightful grandchildren, shortly to be joined by a third.

Meanwhile Judy, feeling thoroughly miserable, rang up Susan Singleton, but was answered by her mother.

"Sue's gone into Stourfield for lunch," Lady Singleton said. "But I think she'll be back fairly early this afternoon. Why not come along directly after lunch and wait for her. I'd love to see you. You haven't been here for ages."

Judy thanked her and rang off. Lady Singleton would be an even better person to consult than Sue, who had only very vague and childish recollections of Celia.

For Judy still thought that the real truth of the whole dreadful business lay in Celia's character and no one yet had presented her with a coherent picture of the woman. Beautiful, yes, they were all agreed on that. Beyond it there was a jumble of contradictory qualities; she was stupid, cunning, dull, nervy, evil, saintly, a coward, a heroine, kind, cruel, gentle, powerful, hypnotic, self-effacing. The list was endless. It didn't make sense.

"No, it doesn't," agreed Lady Singleton.

They were sitting in a small room overlooking the rose garden. The fine summer weather of the week before had broken. A steady rain was bending the heads of the roses in bloom and washing away the black fly and making the dark green leaves shine. The three windows were open top and bottom, but in spite of this it was close in the room. Judy felt it as part of the general oppression under which she lay at the moment. She looked at Lady Singleton, who was gazing out of the window at the falling rain, pleased to think how much tiresome watering she was being saved by the friendly, spilling clouds. She became aware of the girl's eyes fixed on her and turned to her with a smile.

"You believe in Julian, don't you?" she said. "That must be an enormous comfort to him."

"Do you?" Judy asked. Until she knew this, she could not speak freely.

"Yes, I do. I am quite sure he had nothing to do with Celia's death. No, that isn't quite right. He ought not to have loved her, or at least he ought not to have let it grow as it did. But that would be asking too much of him as he was then."

"Tell me about him—then," Judy urged.

"Very young, very unsure of himself, very lost."

"How d'you mean?"

"Lost without a fixed job, fixed hours, fixed pay, all that sort of thing. Very radical views, as all thinking young men have at that stage in their lives. He felt decidedly guilty about living on the capital he'd won, entirely by his own efforts, of course. As we often reminded him. The prize and a government gratuity. But he still felt guilty. I told him Felix had lived all his life, until the war, on money made by his ancestors, but that a large number of other people were living on it too, employed by us. Julian did concede that we didn't waste or throw away anything. He was always interested in the farms and in the tree planting and so on. Until Celia arrived. Then he had no eyes or thoughts for anything else."

"And she?"

"Poor girl," Lady Singleton said, looking out again at the falling drops, "poor girl, she was a born victim."

"How d'you mean?"

"In everything she did she could be both praised and blamed. She always seemed to get into situations where this could happen. I suppose because she had so little initiative. So of course there was more blame than praise. There always is."

"I don't quite see—" Judy found this too complicated.

"Don't you? If people economise aren't they more often blamed for meanness than praised for thrift? If they spend too much they are not called generous, but wasters. And so on. She was in love with Julian. She gave him everything she could

151

and was called wanton. Even Julian thinks of her that way, now."

"Yes, perhaps he does," Judy said, wondering how people thought of herself. Probably not at all, since she didn't live at Upfold, only visited her parents there.

"Poor Julian," Lady Singleton went on. "I hardly recognised him when he came back from London, three weeks after Celia's disappearance. The first thing my husband said was, 'Julian knows where she is.' He didn't, we now discover, but he knew she was dead."

"He will be changed again," Judy said, "when they've stopped suspecting him. I know he's innocent. She must have deceived you all! She certainly bewitched him. I've listened to him talking about her. When he starts he's hating her and all she spoiled for him. Then gradually as he goes on you hear it all changing. So presently she's wonderful, she's a saint, a martyr. I don't know what to think! I'm beginning to hate her too!"

Lady Singleton put out a calming hand and laid it on Judy's arm.

"You mustn't let yourself be jealous of a dead woman, Judy. She was a born victim," she repeated. "We always knew it. It broke our hearts to watch it happening, the village working up as it does from time to time. We began to be afraid of a riot or something more horrible still—a lynching. Felix was prepared to take a gun down in the car and rescue her if anything began to happen."

"It was as serious as *that*?" Judy was incredulous.

"It was indeed. We warned Julian. He had already tried to persuade her to go away with him. That may have helped her to make up her mind."

"Then you believe she really meant to go? Not to escape from Julian and life itself because it had all got too much for her?"

"I'm sure she meant to leave her husband."

Judy sighed.

152

"You liked her, then? You admired her? In spite of her—affair—and ruining Julian?"

"You make it too simple. I loved her beauty. That kind of total loveliness is so rare. It's wholly admirable, whatever the person inside it is like. No, that's wrong. You can't separate a soul from a body. They condition one another from birth. Of course I admired her and liked to see her. There was no question of friendship. We belonged to different generations, with quite different tastes and interests. But she often came to see us here, sometimes alone, sometimes with John."

"Even after she was known to be having an affair with Julian?"

"My dear," Lady Singleton rebuked her. "Everyone did *not* know. Julian was very discreet. If there were snoopers I never came across them. People know I refuse to gossip. I never invited her here with Julian, naturally. She came with John when she did come. My husband knew him in the City."

"Miss Snell thinks she was afraid of Mr Wainwright," Judy said, to keep the focus on Celia.

"Very likely." Lady Singleton was not surprised nor did she seem much impressed. "He was a very positive man. I don't know why I say, was. I believe he came down to the inquest at Stourfield and described how he had tried to find Celia. Not bad for an old man, coming down, I mean."

"He didn't try for very long. He went away to Canada."

"Do you blame him for that? After losing his wife in such mysterious circumstances?"

"I don't know." Judy's voice rose in desperation." I don't know anything, except that I love Julian and believe in him."

"So you should," Lady Singleton told her, giving Judy's hand a friendly pat. "I've told you already I'm positive Julian did nothing to harm her. I think he behaved badly, taking advantage of John, so much older and so much away from home. But nothing more. I'm perfectly sure of that."

Judy did not wait for Susan to come back from Stourfield. She left a message for her and went home. Dr Frost was working in the garden as usual, so Judy went to help him. She was not over fond of gardening but she found it soothing at this troubled time.

Upfold on the whole shared Lady Singleton's view of the case. The village account of Celia's death had always been one of suicide. The more fanciful spirits, led by Mrs Cowley, believed that, being a witch, she had deliberately freed her spirit for more wicked crimes than she had been able to compass in the flesh. The fact that nothing of the sort took place in Upfold after she had gone did not disturb this belief. There was no reason why, being out of the body, she should confine herself to Upfold. There were plenty of crimes in other places to support their conclusions. Those less superstitious thought she had taken her life out of desperation, fear of her husband, fear of her future, fear of Julian's intentions. Everyone knew that her body had been disposed of secretly, though no one except Cutfield and Pawley themselves knew exactly where, until Dr Frost dug her up in his garden. Then everything fell into place.

Upfold resented the fact of the inquest being held in Stourfield. They would have found suicide if they'd had a chance. Even Mr Shalford had guessed that much, frightened as he was of Mrs Cowley's power in the place.

This power now seemed to be coming to an end. On Sunday morning an ambulance drew up at the Winters' house and old Mrs Cowley was carried out, eyes closed, face grey and stern. She had been taken ill in the night and was being removed to Stourfield hospital.

Mr Winter was with her. Dick and the dull girl stood in the doorway for a long time looking after the ambulance. The neighbours did not bother to ask them any questions. They knew already, all Upfold knew, that Mrs Winter had gone off by the London train from Stourfield on Saturday and had not yet come back.

Upfold reserved judgment on these events. But there were many who thought it would not be a bad thing if Mrs Cowley now reached the end of her long life of mischief and worse. At present they kept this thought to themselves. But the old woman's relations and followers were disturbed. Some of them searched out and burned or poured down the sink various little packets of powder and bottles of liquid. Better, they thought, not to keep these by them. Depend on Dr Marshall in future. Not that the effect would be the same. Not by a long chalk.

On Monday Dr Frost had a telephone call from Dr Wallace.

"I'm letting you know this, Harry, as a friendly gesture," Wallace said. "Because that very charming daughter of yours is mixed up with that very foolish young man, who's done his best to land himself in the nick and is still at large through no fault of his own. Now listen. One of those capsules had been very cunningly prepared. The contents of one was the powder prescribed by Marshall for Celia. The other was a solution, a very strong solution, of crude digitalis, mixed with a little of the powder to make it look white from the outside. The digitalis was of a strength to stop the heart's action within a few minutes of being absorbed."

"My God!" Dr Frost exclaimed. "Crude digitalis! What on earth—"

"I think probably only a few of Celia's capsules contained this poison. She may have taken one or two of her real sleeping stuff as well as the lethal dose. Capsules, I need hardly remind you, are made of gelatine and melt quite quickly in the stomach. Drugs in them are absorbed within a quarter of an hour or so."

"Where on earth did the digitalis—?"

"Mitchell is coping with that at the moment. I wondered if you had any ideas?"

Into Dr Frost's mind flashed a picture of foxgloves, but it was vague. So many gardens in Upfold had foxgloves growing in them. His own had a few. He would have to check—

"Not at the moment," he said. "I'll let you know if anything occurs to me."

"Don't keep it to yourself too long," Dr Wallace said. "But I don't think Farnham would know how to produce the stuff, do you?"

CHAPTER XV

Until Dr Wallace's report on the capsules reached Scotland Yard to upset most of his conclusions, Superintendent Mitchell had been satisfied that he was building up a convincing case against Julian. A very strong, very frequent motive was there. Mrs Wainwright had been pregnant, the man had confessed that he knew this. It was not at all uncommon for young men to get rid of their pregnant mistresses. But in addition to this there was his career. These writers were unstable characters on the whole. Farnham had had a perfectly reasonable job in the City with a good salary and very good prospects. He had thrown it up because something he'd written had been given a literary prize. If that wasn't crazy, what was? He hadn't properly made his name yet, he had only this bit of capital and his gratuity. He was exchanging a good source of material, the Superintendent thought with some shrewdness, for solitude and insecurity. Surely not the best atmosphere for producing the 'great novel' he hoped to write.

The Superintendent shook his head over these miscalculations of Julian's, which had been the foundation of all that followed. Of course the evidence was not complete. At present there were too many loopholes for the defence. Those friends of Farnham's in London had sworn now he intended to bring the young woman to their flat. It had been all arranged for him to do so. They had been astonished when they got back from their holiday a week later to find him there alone, thin and pale and distraught, nearly round the bend and quite silent upon the reason for his state, beyond the crude and obvious fact that Celia was *not* there, had not come up with him, had, in fact, vanished.

The latter part of this statement confirmed Mitchell's view that murder had taken place, but the first part denied it. How unlikely that Farnham would make these arrangements for himself and his mistress if he had decided to get rid of her. How unlikely, if it came to that, he would have her in his own house when he administered the sleeping drug or whatever. To have to move her when she was dead seemed totally absurd on the face of it unless, as Farnham swore, her death was a complete surprise to him.

And what of Celia in that case? Had she agreed at last to go away with him? Knowing that Farnham had no means to support her, far less the child as well? Old Wainwright denied that she had asked him for a divorce but said he would not have granted it. He had agreed, after denying it at the inquest, that he was aware of her association with Farnham. He expected it to be temporary. He did not condone it but he realised the discrepancy in their ages.

Mr Wainwright, whom Mitchell had interviewed at the London hotel where he was still staying after the inquest, seemed to be much younger than his actual age, the Superintendent thought. He spoke vigorously and appeared to be entirely sincere. He expressed appropriate horror at the details of Celia's end. This sort of thing would not disappear until science was properly taught in all schools, he said firmly. Upfold could not be blamed entirely for the ignorance of so many of its inhabitants. He hoped Cutfield and Pawley would be punished but not too severely. Cutfield had meant to spare him the shock of discovering his wife's body, but actually her disappearance had caused him much pain and grief.

"You did assume her death in the end, though?" Mitchell said. "Or you would not have married again."

"Quite, quite," the old man answered. "Her family assumed

it when we traced them finally. Did I tell you I was ultimately successful, though not for over a year? For myself I concluded —suicide in some river—the body not appearing—"

"Yes," Mitchell said. "It was reasonable in the circumstances."

This conversation took place on Wednesday, two days after the inquest, but now Dr Wallace had thrown, three days later, a really man-sized spanner in the works with his report on the capsules. Dr Marshall had already stated he had prescribed the soporific found in one of them. The contents of the other were certainly not what he had ordered for either Mr Wainwright, Miss Snell or Mrs Cowley. Theirs had been strong sedatives, of different sorts, nothing whatever to do with digitalis. According to Dr Wallace the substance in the second capsule was not in the pharmacopeia at all. It was a home-brewed lethal dose of poison.

So there he was, back with the village of Upfold, the machinations of the old witch, Mrs Cowley, the hatred built up against Celia. Witch? He caught back the word. This blasted capsule had dragged him into the heart of the business. Death by amateur poison. Who had prepared it, who had administered it?

The original suspects? Hardly that, quite. Farnham's supposed guilt began to fade. He was very unlikely to have known how to make the stuff, though he might have bought it from someone who did. He had access to Celia's capsules.

But then so had others. Wainwright for one, and the daily, Mrs Thompson, for another. Mrs Thompson could be the link with the village enmity. Otherwise wasn't he right back where he had been? He decided to tell Wainwright what Dr Wallace had discovered.

The old man took it quietly. He was silent for a time, then he said, "Mrs Cowley could have made it. She used herbs for many purposes. She had a splendid remedy for warts. I know because I had one Dr Marshall tried to cure. His stuff did no good. Then he sent me to the hospital for a dose of X-ray on the thing. It came back. Our Mrs Thompson suggested Mrs Cowley's stuff. It worked like a charm." He chuckled quietly. "It *was* a charm, I expect. She has a reputation, you know."

Mitchell suppressed a slight revulsion and said, "What else did she make?"

"Cough cures. Embrocations for rheumatism. Ointments for eczema. I must say those weren't as good as the new hydrocortisone. She didn't always win."

"You seem to have made a study of her remedies, sir," Mitchell said.

"Yes." Wainwright looked at him with cool, amused eyes. "Yes, I was interested. She had quite a little laboratory in an old shed behind the Winters' house, where she lives. She showed me her retorts and things. All home-made and very old. Handed down in her family, she said. They were of gypsy origin."

Mitchell had no more questions to ask. He went back to the Yard and rang up Inspector Falk in Stourfield, to announce his intention of coming down that afternoon and also to ask him to visit Mrs Winter's house and investigate the so-called laboratory.

This Inspector Falk did, but Mrs Winter was out for the day, it being Saturday, visiting relatives at Midhurst, Mr Winter said. He took Falk out to the little dark shed, however, where the inspector found a few broken bottles, a gas burner and one or two pestles and mortars of very ancient design. There were no medicinal preparations either in process of being made or in containers. There was no evidence that Mrs Cowley or anyone else had performed any chemical operations there at any time.

"She used to brew up one or two things when she was younger," Mr Winter said, in an all too offhand manner. "But not for many years now."

Mrs Cowley said the same, repeating over and over again that Inspector Falk could go round Upfold house by house and they'd stand by the truth of what she said. He had no doubt of it. But he was not altogether surprised when he learned on Sunday that she had been taken to Stourfield hospital that morning following a heart attack in the night that might prove to be fatal.

Rumours began to flash about Upfold, gaining a more and more lurid aspect as they grew. Julian, who had returned to the village on Friday night, was seen again by Mitchell. He was asked a searching string of questions about his knowledge of drugs, the number and nature of those in his possession at the time of Celia's death, his knowledge of chemistry, if any, his dealings, if any, with Mrs Cowley. All this in addition to questions and severe censure on the subject of the two capsules he had failed to produce at the inquest.

He came out of all this tolerably well. He had never been to the Winters' house nor had dealings of any kind with Mrs Cowley. There were plenty of people in Upfold to support him in this. Mitchell knew he would get no further by direct questioning. He was no more successful with Miss Snell.

"It looks as if the village was responsible for Celia's death, after all," Dr Frost said, as he and his wife, having done some shopping in the village and noting the withdrawn manner of the people, went back towards their parked car.

"Which is what we always thought," Mrs Frost reminded him. "Oh, there's Mrs Graveney! I wonder if she knows how Mrs Cowley is today."

They moved towards her, since she was alone and had always been so eager to cultivate their friendship. But when she saw them she smiled bleakly and turning away hurried off towards the car park.

"Well!" said Mrs Frost. "What's the matter with her, I should like to know?"

"We may find more of that," Dr Frost said, sadly. "The Upfold social sphere is resentful. Haven't you noticed? As we get nearer the truth everyone is afraid of what it may prove to be. And we started it. Or rather, I did. A newcomer, turning up a big stinking heap of scandal and crime right under their noses. It will take time for them to forgive us."

Mrs Frost was alarmed.

"You wouldn't think of leaving?" she asked, with a quiver in her voice. "I do love Mulberry Cottage so much."

"Of course not. Who cares what the Graveneys think? The Singletons are on our side."

"Snob!" said Mrs Frost, laughing.

Dr Frost drove to the Stourfield Hospital and flourishing his medical status boldly was allowed to speak first to the Sister of the ward where Mrs Cowley lay; next to the consultant physician who was making his round of the ward, and finally, by his permission, to Mrs Cowley. Mrs Frost, in the background, but keeping close to her husband, was also admitted into the curtained cubicle.

"Do you remember me, Mrs Cowley?" she asked, gently.

The old woman was sitting up, supported by many pillows. Her breathing was quiet now, her face pale but quite peaceful. Her small dark eyes, very much alive, darted from one to the other of her visitors.

"Wot d'you want from me?" she asked. Her voice, weaker than when Mrs Frost had first seen her, was still harsh.

"I want you to tell me about the herbal medicines you make," Dr Frost said. "I'm a doctor and I'm very interested."

The old woman turned her eyes on him. There was laughter in them and spite and a kind of wicked triumph.

"You're the one that dug 'er up, ain't yer?" she said.

"Yes."

So it was to be cards on the table, Dr Frost thought and the strongest nerve wins. And by God, she's got a nerve, he decided, staring at the bold ancient face on the pillows.

"Yes," he repeated. "Did you make up the capsules for her yourself or did you only brew the poison?"

That shook her. She began to tremble all over. Then she whispered, furiously, "Go away! D'you want to kill me? Go away, the both of yer. Sister! Sister!"

Her voice was too low to be heard outside the cubicle.

Mrs Frost half rose, saying hurriedly, "Shall I get Sister?"

"Sit down," said Dr Frost.

He leaned forward, placing his hand on Mrs Cowley's wrist.

"I am a doctor," he repeated. "I know that you are very ill, very ill indeed."

"I'm better. They done me good. If I stay quiet—not get upset—"

"You will last a little longer. But not very long, Mrs Cowley. Not if you have to go to prison for the murder of Mrs Wainwright."

He was taking a calculated risk and he knew it. If he had judged her right she would fight. She could be angry, but never really afraid.

"I never! You lying old bastard! Think I care? You can't prove nothing!"

That was true, unless others helped her in making her nostrums.

"We can and we shall. You didn't work it all alone. Your daughters helped you—"

"They never helped me. I shut them out. They were no good. I had the knowledge. They weren't fit to get it, not any one of them."

"Who gave you the knowledge?"

"My granny," she said, proudly, lifting her head from the pillows. "She had it from her mother. We've always 'ad it. For warts, for the cough in the consumption, for the rheumatics—"

"Go on."

She was staring beyond him now, seeing herself the healer, the tribal doctor, the priestess, the giver of life and death. "There's a salve for the itch, but that's not asked for so much these days."

"Thanks to hygiene. Go on."

"There's the drops for sore eyes. There's the love potions." She gave a lewd sideways glance at Mrs Frost who shrank back in her chair.

162

"And the death potions?" said Dr Frost.

That touched her. For a moment her face collapsed, her eyes closed.

"Oh, Harry, be careful!" Mrs Frost breathed.

But the old woman rallied. Dr Frost had his fingers on her pulse again. It was steady, reasonably full.

"Why did you make that poison?" he demanded. "Some of the blue capsules have been found. We know what was in them."

The dark eyes flashed.

"The fool! Left some about, did 'e? The fool!"

"Who? Who did you give them to? Tell me."

"Him that first put it in my mind she were a witch. 'My wife is a witch, Mrs Cowley', 'e said. When 'e come for my wart cure. A witch. It warn't long before they all come to believe it."

Dr Frost put out a hand to subdue his wife's rising excitement.

"Surely he only meant it as a joke?" he said.

"Oh, no. It warn't no joke. 'E wanted to be rid of 'er."

"On account of Mr Farnham?" Dr Frost was prepared to be quite reckless now. "He was jealous?"

"'E said that long afore Mr Farnham took up with 'er. It's my belief they didn't 'it it off together. Their ages—"

"Yes, yes. But it was *before* Mr Farnham came on the scene? Is that what you're saying?"

He cursed himself for not making a table of dates for all the events of Celia's tragic life at Upfold.

Mrs Cowley nodded. But she could not be right, he thought. Julian had fallen for Celia as soon as she arrived. Dr Frost could see she was boasting now of her own powers. He had been right. She was not afraid. She had been angry. Now she was complacent. He recalled her to the realities of the situation as she had put it.

"Are you really saying that Mr Wainwright was anxious to get rid of his wife even before Mr Farnham knew her?"

"That's right. 'E thought she'd go, with everyone making it so unpleasant for 'er."

"Unpleasant!" His fury at this description of the persecution nearly broke out in curses.

"But she wouldn't take the 'int," Mrs Cowley concluded. "Not even when the brat was on the way."

There was nothing the village had not known. He thought of Dr Marshall's reticence and felt a kind of despair at this disparity between professional standards and brute behaviour. But remembering human frailty and his own he soon felt inclined to laugh bitterly instead.

"Mrs Cowley," he said, as sternly as he could. "An innocent man is suspected because you have kept silent about your crimes. Do you realise that you can be accused of helping a murderer?"

She was not impressed.

"Get along with you, you old meddler," she said. "D'you think I'd 'ave told you if I thought any of yous could prove it? Get along with you. And you too, missus." She turned fiercely on Mrs Frost. "Staring like a rude child as you did that time you brought your bits of washing to my daughter."

"You haven't seen your daughter since you came here, have you?" said Mrs Frost, saying the first thing that came to her. "You know she hasn't come back to Upfold since Saturday, don't you?"

This time Mrs Cowley's collapse was not partially feigned. They called the Sister, who drove them out of the ward with reproaches for upsetting her patient.

"You shouldn't have said that," Dr Frost remarked, as they drove away.

"I couldn't help it. She was so *awful*!"

"Yes. But we don't want her to die. Not yet."

As he drove into Upfold, Dr Frost turned off to pass the Winters' house. The dull girl was hanging over the gate. Dr Frost stopped the car and leaned out.

"Has your mother come home yet?" he called.

164

"Mind yer own business," the girl answered.

"I am. I want my last week's washing. Is it ready yet?"

"I dunno. Mum's not 'ere."

"Can you remember to tell your father I called and why?"

"Dad's not 'ere, neether."

Dr Frost drove on. Mrs Frost said, "Was there any point in speaking to that poor creature?"

"Not much, perhaps. It was mainly an excuse for looking into their garden. They have a fine cluster of foxglove plants."

"I could have told you that. I think I did, actually. A lovely clump of foxgloves and delphiniums. I'm sure I told you."

"I had no reason to remember it, then," sighed Dr Frost, feeling suddenly very tired indeed.

He rang up Stourfield police station that evening and was asked to speak to Superintendent Mitchell. The latter already knew of Dr Frost's visit to the hospital. With his sergeant he had gone over all the ground Falk had covered on Saturday, and had checked at various houses in Upfold the truth of Wainwright's description of Mrs Cowley's activities. The hospital staff had refused to allow him to see Mrs Cowley. He was indignant when Dr Frost told him about his conversation earlier that day with the old woman.

"Why the devil didn't they let me see her, then?" he demanded.

"Perhaps because I happen to be a doctor."

"You got all this out of her, none of it written down, no corroboration?"

"My wife was present."

"It isn't evidence," Mitchell groaned. "It wouldn't stand up in court."

"I'm afraid she isn't likely to make a signed statement to you or anyone official. She spoke freely to me because she felt safe in doing so."

"I'll have to see her and try."

"Perhaps Mrs Winter would talk. She may have had no part in it."

"Mrs Winter hasn't turned up yet. I'm looking for her."

"You can see Wainwright again. Tell him Mrs Cowley has confessed. At least to supplying him with a poisonous dose of digitalis. Get his reaction to that."

There was a moment's silence on the line. Then the Superintendent's voice came again, stern and official.

"I'd be obliged, doctor, if you would kindly leave the conduct of this case in my hands." Annoyance broke through dignity. "If you go on interfering this way you're likely to get into trouble—serious trouble—for obstructing the police in the execution of their duty."

"Nonsense," said Dr Frost, not at all put out. "I've told you every single thing exactly as it happened. And very promptly, too."

He replaced the receiver before the astounded Superintendent could make an appropriate reply.

CHAPTER XVI

Upfold was still divided, but the general opinion was hardening in favour of the writer. After all, the majority of the villagers had never believed in supernatural powers and manifestations. Their dislike of Celia had been based mainly on their total misunderstanding of her character and behaviour. She was indeed a stranger in their midst and remained so. They had been perfectly willing to let the fanatical minority persecute and vilify her because in that way they hoped she would leave the place. They had heard, but had shut their minds against, the manner of that leaving. They approved the result, let the method stay hidden.

Now the situation was reversed. Upfold was getting into the news in a very unpleasant manner. Dr Frost had started it, but it all seemed to be the fault of Mrs Cowley, who had kept them in fear for so many years. Memories of her earlier misdeeds, unrelated to Mrs Wainwright, began to circulate. The searchlight of suspicion was turned on the house of Winter and Mrs Winter had not yet come home.

But though Upfold continued to be chilly towards the Frosts, considering them responsible for the present unpleasantness and publicity affecting the whole village, the Singletons continued to show them friendliness and sympathy. Sir Felix called on Dr Frost on Monday evening, chiefly to say that he and his wife were only too grateful for all the doctor had done. Grateful in his turn, Dr Frost described the present position in the inquiry.

"I see no point in being secret over it," he said. "After all, the village keeps itself abreast of the investigation by its own methods, so why shouldn't we?"

"Exactly," said Sir Felix and went on to tell Dr Frost all he knew about Wainwright.

"I've known him for years," he said. "Well, to be exact, ever since I accepted a directorship in the City when I left the army after the war. He'd spent the best part of his life in Canada, but after the war he promoted a subsidiary company of his Canadian business in England and more or less based himself on this country, though I believe he had interests in France, too. My concern had dealings with him and that was how I got to know him."

"He can't have been a young man, then," Dr Frost remarked.

"He wasn't. Far from it. But he looked quite fifteen years younger than his age and behaved like it, too."

"So I gather."

"Of course he had phenomenal luck with his business. It was touch and go with him for a long time. He might have lost everything he'd built up in Canada. He went over there when he was thirty-five, you know. After pretty well failing in various jobs over here, I was told, though I can't vouch for that. He always said he went because he was browned off with our English ways of business. But he made quite a fortune in the twenty years he was there before he decided to expand still further."

"He doesn't sound really very competent," Dr Frost said. "How did he manage to get started in Canada? Did he ever tell you that?"

"No. But he used to refer occasionally to a partner. I expect he found someone who was willing to use his flair, which was quite genuine, mind you, and back it with the needed capital."

"And stop him throwing away the results, recklessly?"

"Perhaps."

"What sort of man is he?" Dr Frost asked, to carry the conversation further. "We have a very muddled picture of him in this case. Some people think Celia was frightened of him."

"Who?"

"Miss Snell, actually."

"Oh, that woman!" Sir Felix looked very disapproving. "A crackpot, if ever there was one."

"I think perhaps only an artist with much ambition and not a very robust talent," said Dr Frost, mildly.

Sir Felix gave him a sharp look.

"You may be right. You're used to making a diagnosis, aren't you?"

Dr Frost ignored this. He went on, thoughtfully, "Then again, Wainwright seems to have ignored his wife's affair with Julian, even condoned it positively."

"I doubt that. He may have controlled his feelings for various reasons, but I know he's quick-tempered, proud, jealous, full of energy, even ready for violence in upholding his rights."

"In the business world, you mean?"

"I imagine he would hardly be likely to display quite opposite characteristics in his private life."

Dr Frost sighed. It was all very confusing. The picture of Wainwright that Sir Felix presented fitted the suspicion that it was he who had put the poison capusles in his wife's bottle of sleeping drugs. According to Mrs Cowley he had bought her wart cure. So he knew of her medical activities. But how to prove it? How to prove that Julian had not gone to the old woman instead? She had implied that it was Wainwright but she might have done that on purpose to mislead him.

"Did you see Wainwright at all when he was in Stourfield?" he asked. "At the inquest?"

"I made a point of seeing him in London after the case," Sir Felix answered. "We didn't ask him to come down to Upfold, knowing what the village thought of him after the inquest."

"They think now he neglected her, don't they? The more sensible ones, I mean."

"Yes. But the others, the crazy ones, think he aided and abetted her wicked spells."

"How deluded can you get!" sighed the doctor.

"You should know. Anyway, he seemed very much his old self to me. Rather shockingly so, I felt, in view of the ghastly revelations we'd heard. I didn't stay with him long. He was looking a bit frayed. Not surprising. I understood he was going home to Cornwall today."

"How did he come to Stourfield?" Dr Frost asked. "I left the court before he did."

"A car, chauffeur driven. I was surprised. He was a keen driver when he lived here. Drove a Bentley himself, up to London and back every week. Celia had her own car—don't remember the make—something small."

Dr Frost was surprised.

"I was told he always went up by train," he said. "No one mentioned his own car. The garage wouldn't take two."

"No. No, you're right. The Bentley stood in the drive. They always used it over the weekends. Perhaps he just took it in to Stourfield station and parked it there midweek. But he gave me to understand he was never so happy as when he was travelling at eighty on a good road."

"Yes," said Dr Frost. A new picture of Wainwright was emerging; not a very truthful man, able to put anything across. The con man of police records. Had he one? Was that at the bottom of it all?

"He would be feeling his age by now," the doctor suggested. "And perhaps the agitation of this whole business. Or he may always have a chauffeur now. It's ten years later."

"I doubt it," Sir Felix said. "I doubt it very much."

That night there was a thunderstorm over Upfold. It had threatened all day, moving in dark clouds over the village towards the downs, then circling back to cover the sky again. It broke with unexpected violence about midnight, raged for half an hour in noisy crashes with pelting rain and then passed on, leaving the disturbed inhabitants in peace for the rest of the night.

Dr Frost was up early, anxious to discover if any damage had been done to his garden. Rain was needed, but thunderdrops were not the most welcome form of it.

Mrs Frost slept later. When she did rouse herself, heavy-eyed and dry-mouthed, she was annoyed to see that the storm had brought down a shower of black drops from the chimney of her room on to the hearth behind her electric fire and also some lumps from the chimney brickwork. She went downstairs to get the breakfast, thinking it was most unfair to have thunderstorm havoc to deal with on a day when Mrs Thompson would not be there.

Dr Frost came in from the garden when she called him.

"Wonderfully little damage," he said, cheerfully, as he pulled off his gardening boots in the back porch and put on his carpet slippers.

"You're lucky. My grate upstairs is a perfect shambles."

"I'll help you," he said.

When he came to look at it he saw at once that the storm had placed a further piece in the jigsaw of Celia's death.

"Doesn't this remind you of anything?" he said, breaking

up a small lump of plaster that had rolled out on to the carpet. "Greyish-yellow crumbly dust. No?"

Mrs Frost stared. She did remember. The first night at Mulberry Cottage. The queer substance on her bed.

"I didn't tell you at the time," Dr Frost went on, "because I didn't want to upset you. But I saw footprints round by the coal-shed and it seemed to me possible that someone had climbed into the house by the bathroom window and had come into this room."

"We couldn't think where the stuff had come from because the whole house had just been re-decorated."

"Exactly. We didn't think of the chimney."

"Someone came in to find something in the chimney."

"Yes. There was only your electric fire in the grate to move away and move back. But perhaps some chimney plaster fell then and though they cleaned it up a little fell on the bed, unnoticed."

Mrs Frost was looking rather pale.

"I don't see why—" she said, gulped a little and went on. "I don't see why they had to come *after* we got here. I mean, the house was empty all those years—"

Dr Frost considered this.

"I know. But if you remember there was a gas fire fixed in this grate. We had it taken away, didn't we?"

"So we did. That lets out Snowthorne," Mrs Frost said, briskly. She had apparently recovered from the first unpleasant shock. "And Cutfield too, I suppose. If he'd wanted to find something—they're related, aren't they? It wouldn't be—it wouldn't be—?"

Her face had gone pale again.

"It wasn't the missing head, if that's what you're thinking," Dr Frost said brutally, to stop the rising hysteria he saw in his wife's face. "And I'm sure neither Cutfield nor Pawley would ever dream of climbing in that way again. It's just an obvious route. Anyone would use it. That's why I always fasten the bathroom window when we're out."

171

"What we'll have to know," said Mrs Frost with an effort, "is when the gas fire was put in. I mean if Celia had it—"

"She couldn't have hidden something in the chimney that someone afterwards wanted to get at," finished Dr Frost. "I'll ask Alford if he knows."

Mr Alford, distinctly mystified, supplied the information. All the grates had been old-fashioned, open ones in the Wainwrights' time. He agreed that there had been a gas fire in the front bedroom when the house finally fell empty. He supposed that Mr Wainwright's tenants had put it in.

Dr Frost thanked him and went on to consult the local branch of the Gas Board. Records at this source were more difficult to tap. He was advised to make an application in writing, but having refused firmly to do so a young, unhardened assistant consented to look up the dates of their fitter's visits to Mulberry Cottage. A small bribe from Dr Frost helped the investigation, together with the fact that the office was slack in the summer months. He had his answer the next day. The gas had been connected in the bedroom a week after the arrival of Wainwright's successors. It had been disconnected at the main when they left.

"So that's that," Dr Frost told his wife on his return from Stourfield. "Slow off the mark at the beginning, or possibly they didn't want to get at the thing to begin with. Who came in and what for is another question. And why? Most important of all, that. I doubt if we shall get an answer to it."

If he did not get immediate answers to his questions Dr Frost did have pointers and that within a few hours of expressing his frustration.

During the storm a tramp had been on the road a couple of miles away from Upfold. He was one of the regulars who travelled all the summer months between Stourfield and Midhurst, spending a night or two at the Reception Centre in each town. If the weather was really fine he slept out, but on the whole he preferred the comfort of a dormitory bed at the Centre, even though it meant enduring the compulsory bath that went with it.

The storm had taken him unawares. He had decided to spend that night under the stars and had turned away from his usual route to follow the lanes under the downs. The evening was close, his progress slow. He rested frequently and coming to a quarry at about six that evening, decided to stay there for the night. A little hut in the quarry, set back in an overhang, made a kind of recess in which he could lie. The hut was locked. He considered breaking in to take any valuables it contained, but gave up the idea. He knew of no market for explosives, nor did he like the idea of handling them.

He was tired from walking all day and slept heavily for some hours. The storm woke him. On the floor of the quarry the noise of thunder echoing round the hollow appalled him. The rain soaked him to the skin in a few minutes. Cursing wildly, he snatched up his bundle, scrambled to his feet and stared wildly about him. The lightning flashes showed him a clump of bushes on the other side of the quarry. Trees, he knew, were dangerous in thunderstorms, but bushes? Surely not. He stumbled across and forced his way in, crawling deeper and deeper until he was brought up short by an obstruction over which he collapsed on his face. The obstruction was the body of Mrs Winter.

He did not know this at the time. He knew only the panic of his discovery and the confusion of mind it caused. Should he go on and say nothing? That would be crazy. There were signs of his presence he could not destroy. He had done quite a bit of damage to the bushes for a start. That looked bad— suggested a struggle. In the end he did the most sensible thing; he walked into Upfold and roused Constable Galton. The latter, being a considerate man, gave the terrified soaked creature a dry shirt and some old trousers for a start, made his wife get up to brew tea and went off to the quarry on his bicycle. By the light of his torch he identified Mrs Winter.

She seemed to have been dead for some time; she was cold and limp and discoloured. There was a scarf tied tightly round her neck.

He did not touch her but rode back to report. The tramp was reassured. He had left Midhurst the morning before, the warden there could testify. Mrs Winter had been gone from Upfold three days.

She had indeed been murdered, strangled with her own scarf which was identified by her shocked, trembling husband. He would say nothing except that he had been afraid of this ever since he had found out, on Sunday evening, that she had not been to her relations at all.

"Why didn't you report that?" Mitchell demanded.

Winter was silent. The question was repeated.

"Thought she'd be back. No call to interfere. Old enough to look after 'erself. Got me own work to attend to." The answers were wrung out of him with difficulty.

"Don't you know where she went? She was on the London train. You knew that, didn't you?"

He nodded. It was common knowledge, useless to deny it.

"Was that how she'd travel to Midhurst? Didn't she usually go by bus?"

No answer.

"Who was she going to see in London? Was it Mr Wain-wright?"

"If you bloody well know the answers why ask me?"

"So it *was* Mr Wainwright?"

"I don't know, I tell you!" Winter was suddenly voluble, protesting. "I swear to God I never interfered. She and 'er Ma, they were a pair! I never interfered. That's gospel. Much as my life was worth. Ask the old bitch! She's at the bottom of it all. I never knew nothing! You got to believe me. Nothing!"

It seemed very probable. But when Mitchell arrived at the hospital shortly after, it was to learn that Mrs Cowley had passed into a coma and was not likely to recover from it.

"You reported she was improving," he said reproachfully to the ward Sister.

"She rallied wonderfully," Sister answered. "She had a little setback after Dr Frost was with her yesterday, but she got over that, too. Though she had a restless night. Early this morning she was asking for her daughter, Mrs Winter. We had to say she wasn't home yet."

"Had to say? Did you know Mrs Winter was dead?"

"Yes. The constable at Upfold rang up to say so and that Mr Winter couldn't come as he had to interview the police."

"You didn't tell Mrs Cowley that?"

"Oh, no. I'm afraid that was the grandchildren. They came quite early. I warned them not to speak about it, but the young man, Dick, was very jittery, though I think he understood. It was the girl who told her. At least—"

"Well?"

"I sent a nurse into the cubicle with them," said Sister, "but the girl just blurted it out. She's a bit mental, you know, I don't think she could help it. She doesn't usually speak at all with strangers present. That's why I asked nurse—"

"Yes, yes."

"But it seems Mrs Cowley fixed her with those wicked little eyes of hers and made her say what she knew. Then the old woman just lay back and—seemed to give up trying to live."

Mitchell cursed himself for spending so long, so unprofitably with Winter when Mrs Cowley should have been his first concern. But he knew she would not have told him anything. Dr Frost had been right there.

So he was left with suspicions and a very slender chance of justifying them. Had Mrs Winter gone to London to blackmail Wainwright? Perhaps. What had she got to threaten him with? Just the knowledge of the digitalis preparation, the fact that it had been made, the fact that he had bought it from Mrs Cowley?

He could laugh at that now. There was no possible proof.

175

What else? Mitchell had no idea and Wainwright had gone home to Cornwall. Nevertheless he could perhaps discover if he had had any visitors at his London hotel over the weekend. And if he had taken out a car himself during Saturday or Sunday. There was a vague case now against Wainwright, but no adequate motive. Jealousy, pride? Not really, with a man like him. He had no police record, but one or two accounts of his early business transactions, before he went to Canada had been very near the borderline of legality.

Mitchell did not share Sir Felix's views. He thought Wainwright would put his general interests, his personal position, his own safety, far above any emotional considerations. He might have wanted to drive Celia away in order to divorce her for desertion instead of adultery. He had been a patient man in his long-term business deals. Patient and ruthless. It would operate in his private life, too. But murder? And murder again to avoid discovery? There was nothing so far to justify it.

Mitchell went back to London. The motive, the justification he sought, was lying on his desk at Scotland Yard.

CHAPTER XVII

Mrs Thompson was packing a clean overall into her large string bag before setting off for work on Wednesday morning when Dr Frost drove up to her house. Being in the kitchen she did not see him until he appeared at her back door.

"I should like to have a few words with you, Mrs Thompson," he said, solemnly.

She was awed into letting him come in and stood waiting.

"May we sit down?" asked Dr Frost, fixing her with a steady gaze. "First of all I am going to tell you a story."

Mrs Thompson began to quake inwardly, but she summoned up all her courage and said, "I've my work to go to. Mrs Frosts's expecting me."

"I will not keep you long."

Dr Frost told her about the footsteps in the dew, the open bathroom window, the chimney plaster dust on Mrs Frost's bed. He reminded her of the types of heating in that room. The Wainwrights had kept an open grate. Was it ever used for a fire?

"Never," said Mrs Thompson, wondering how much the doctor now knew or guessed.

"Was the room never heated, even in the winter?"

"Not to my knowledge. It wasn't much used, not that room."

"I understood it was Mrs Wainwright's bedroom?"

"She moved in there that last summer. They had the double bed before."

"I see. So even in October when she died she still had an open grate in her bedroom?"

"To the best of my knowledge. I wasn't there evenings."

"But you were there every morning at that time, weren't you? And you knew that grate very well."

"I don't know what you mean by that," said Mrs Thompson, rising. "I didn't ask you to come here. I'll be getting off to my work. You could've spoken to me there."

"Sit down," said Dr Frost.

Mrs Thompson sank back into her chair. She was really frightened now, thinking of the murdered Mrs Winter, news of whose death had flashed round the village at dawn the day before, wondering, too, what old Mrs Cowley had confessed to.

"What do you think was hidden in that chimney?" he said. "Who did you tell? Who came to find it the evening we moved in?"

"Not *me*!" said Mrs Thompson, her voice rising. "I swear it wasn't me."

"No," said Dr Frost. "I don't suppose it was. You wouldn't have climbed into the house, I'm sure. But it was the way Cutfield and Pawley got in wasn't it? So somebody thought of copying them."

"What would they want so long after?" asked Mrs Thompson, rallying. "If there'd bin anything to get it'd 'ave gone when she did."

"Oh, no. Those two who mutilated and buried her made no search of the room. They had no time—no object in doing so. Mr Farnham stayed only long enough to put the body in the bed. We have those other two as witnesses of that. You were locked out next morning. When Mr Wainwright, left, as he did at once, the house was locked up and remained so."

"Them others come," Mrs Thompson said, obstinately. "I give them three mornings, as you very well know."

"But they had a gas fire installed in that room before you started work there again, hadn't they? Whatever it was you'd put in the chimney—"

"I never! She kept it there herself. Part of her devilment! Spells and that!"

"Is that true? Did you read it, whatever it was?"

Mrs Thompson gave up. She began to dab at her eyes and blow her nose. Her voice sank to an ignominious whine.

"I don't read handwriting that good. I couldn't make it out. It was like a diary—"

"I expect it was a diary."

"I caught 'er one day putting it up the chimney. She didn't see me. Hiding it from *him*, I suppose."

"And the last time you saw her do it was the day before she died."

"That was the only time. She was worried that day. She warn't so careful as usual."

Dr Frost nodded.

"Now we're getting somewhere. Did it never occur to

178

you to tell Mr Wainwright about this—diary, you call it. A book, I suppose?"

"Sort of a book. With dates. Small. Red cover."

"Why didn't you tell him? Everyone thought she'd gone away and that might have helped him to find her, mightn't it?"

Mrs Thompson said nothing.

"Or did you know, even then, that she had *not* gone away?"

"Yes."

"You knew or you guessed?"

"Guessed."

"Why? What made you so certain?"

Mrs Thompson's head drooped. She spoke now hardly above a whisper.

"On account of what Mrs Winter gave me to give to 'im."

"Ah!"

So it was out at last and Dr Frost took no time at all in forcing details from Mrs Thompson. She was abject now, the guilt of years pressing on her, though she swore over and over again that she had no part in it except as a messenger. No part, no suspicion of evil, no thought of revenge? Well, she was a stupid, ignorant woman. The lost husband must have had the brains that had betrayed the wretched son. It was possible she did not really understand what she was doing.

"Did Mrs Winter say what was in the package?"

"Mrs Cowley's cough cure. For himself."

"Just that?"

She nodded.

"You were to give it into his hands?"

"When 'e was alone, yes."

She might have guessed—she must have guessed. But she would stick to her story. She believed it now, after all these years.

"And you told Mrs Winter about the little red book?"

"Yes, I told 'er."

Dr Frost waited for her to pull herself together, then he spoke again.

"You will have to tell all this to the police," he said. "It's no use crying, Mrs Thompson. Don't you see, it's vital in finding out who murdered Mrs Winter. She must have got hold of that book, probably young Dick climbed in for it. She was trying to blackmail the murderer of Mrs Wainwright and he killed her."

"Mr Wainwright killed her?"

"Isn't that obvious? Didn't you believe that, yourself?"

"I never saw 'e 'ad any call to. Divorce 'er, that's wot we all thought 'e'd do. Not that we cared so long as she left."

The old spite was back now. Mrs Thompson got up.

"I'm going," she said. "After the way I've been abused— Making me late, too—"

"Nonsense," said Dr Frost. "I'll drive you to Stourfield, to see Superintendent Mitchell. If you won't come I'll ring him up and you'll have him looking for you at your work."

"Threats now!" said Mrs Thompson. "Let me tell you, I'm not afraid of wot you say. Nosy old bastard! It's the last time I ever set foot in Mulberry Cottage so you may as well know it."

"I'm sorry," said Dr Frost, moving to the door. "I only hope you won't regret it. You'd find it much the wisest thing to do."

But Mrs Thompson had slammed the back door on him and it is doubtful if she heard this last piece of advice.

"Will you really leave her to think it over?" Mrs Frost asked, when the doctor returned, undecided now whether to tell the police himself or give Mrs Thompson a chance to do so. "She hasn't come here. It definitely points to Wainwright, doesn't it?"

"He shouldn't have killed Mrs Winter. I suppose she tried to blackmail him with the diary. Pity Mrs Thompson is so illiterate. I wonder if she was to get a rake-off and only pretended not to know what was in it."

"Oh, dear," said Mrs Frost. "It all gets worse and worse, doesn't it? That packet might have really been cough cure. Anyone could have bought the digitalis from Mrs Cowley. How do we really know Julian didn't buy medicines from the old woman? She never really told you, did she?"

"No," said Dr Frost. "That's why I'm going to Cornwall today to speak to Wainwright himself."

"You can't! It's much too far!"

"Nonsense. I shall fly down from London. I shall stay at a hotel there tonight. I can see him this evening if I start at once."

Mrs Frost gave up. There was only one way to prevent him going and that was by warning the police of his intention. But she could not bring herself to do this. Nor even to tell them about Mrs Thompson. That woman's evidence could keep, Harry had said. So Mrs Frost spent a miserable day, growing more and more anxious until, after retiring to bed at ten o'clock she was roused by the telephone bell an hour later to find her husband speaking from his hotel room in Helston, to tell her the case was over and she must bring the car to Stourfield to meet his train down from London. He would be leaving early next morning by air. He would let her know what time to meet him.

Dr Frost had succeeded beyond his expectation. He had called, without warning, at the address he found in the Fowey hotel directory. The front door was opened by an elderly woman, stout, grey-haired, with a good-natured homely face rather heavily powdered.

"Mrs Wainwright?" asked Dr Frost.

"Yes?"

"I wonder if I could see your husband for a few minutes?"

Her face clouded with suspicion.

"Who are you?" she asked, bluntly. "The police? The press?"

She had a marked Canadian accent, Dr Frost noticed. So he would expect. She had married Wainwright in Canada after he returned there and had come over to spend his retirement with him here in Trethuan.

"Neither," he said. "I'm Dr Frost, who bought Mulberry Cottage from him."

"Come in," she said, at once. He followed her into a pleasant room, over-filled with furniture. Some of it was modern, most of it heavily Victorian, none of it valuable, he thought, a little surprised, seeing that Wainwright had been a very wealthy man for a good many years.

Mrs Wainwright did not ask him to sit down. She closed the door and turning to him again said, "So it was you caused all this trouble we've been having. Pity you didn't leave well alone."

Dr Frost was nettled.

"If you call it well to have a murder lie undiscovered and a murderer go scot free—"

"What good will it do to put that poor young man in prison for life?"

Dr Frost caught back a declaration of Julian's innocence.

"Would it be possible for me to see your husband for a few minutes, Mrs Wainwright?"

"He's resting." She hesitated, then went on. "He's not been himself since he had to attend that inquest. He should have come straight back. Not stayed in London the whole week. It's knocked him up. He's feeling his age."

"I'm sure he found it trying."

"What d'you want to see him about?"

It was Dr Frost's turn to hesitate. Then he said, "Have you read the newspaper today, Mrs Wainwright?"

"No. At least, not all through. Why?"

"There has been a second murder in Upfold. Of a woman who probably knew the truth of the first. The police are investigating. There are one or two aspects of this new case and of the old that the police don't know, but which I do.

I think Mr Wainwright should hear what I have to say to him."

She began to look troubled at last. Not afraid, but perplexed, uncertain how to act.

"Do you think he will refuse to see me?" Dr Frost said, gently.

"Refuse? John? You bet he won't. Hasn't he always played his hunches, recklessly, foolishly, half the time. His flair, he calls it."

She was panting a little, she had spoken so fast. Her anxiety had brushed aside her usual level-headed caution.

"D'you think he'd have done as well as he did without me to back him up and hold him back? Why, he came over without a penny to his name!"

Dr Frost understood at last. Now everything fell into place. Here was the motive, standing beside him, betraying the husband she had loved, supported, controlled, encouraged, for so long. And now had ruined, without hope of recovery.

"Were you shocked when you read about Celia in the newspaper? Or did your husband tell you about her first?"

"I've always known he liked the girls," she answered, biting her lip. "I wasn't exactly a beauty queen, even when I was young. But if you think I minded what happened to that tart—calling herself Mrs Wainwright—then—"

A voice from the doorway said, with harsh emphasis, "You silly bitch! Why can't you ever hold your tongue at the right time?"

John Wainwright came into the room. He caught his wife's wrist in a grip that made her gasp and turned her round without any noticeable effort.

"Scram!" he said.

She went without a word. Only as she closed the door behind her Dr Frost heard her break into noisy crying. Wainwright paid no attention whatever.

"Sit down," he said. "So you're Frost, are you?"

"How long have you been listening?" the doctor asked.

"From the start. Don't let it worry you. I'd have stopped her earlier if I'd realised what your little game was."

"I played no little game. I had no idea until she made it obvious that you've been married to her for so long. How long, exactly?"

"Two years after I went to Canada in the first place. So what?"

"So your marriage to Celia was bigamous?"

"She doesn't know that—not yet. I hoped to spare her. She's been good to me. She knows—I go off the rails now and then. She thinks Celia just called herself Mrs to set her right with the neighbours."

"Mrs Wainwright will have to know. The police will tell her."

"If you think you're going to tell them—"

Dr Frost brushed aside the threat, wondering if he was capable of tackling this old man fifteen years his senior whose strong hands were opening and shutting most menacingly.

"Why did you marry Celia?" he said.

"She wouldn't let me have her unless. I thought she was after the money. Well, with that face and figure who'd have thought she'd be a virgin at twenty-five?"

"Not your type, certainly."

Wainwright swallowed that. He was holding in his rage, Dr Frost knew, until he found out what the latter had come for.

"So you married her," Dr Frost went on. "Why did you want to get rid of her?"

"Connie was complaining again. Never liked me to stay too long in England."

"Had you been over before, then?"

"Twice."

"You haven't disclosed that to Sir Felix, have you? Far less the police?"

"No. Certainly not."

"So you had to go back to Canada and get rid of Celia

184

in order to do so. You couldn't divorce her, without exposing yourself or risking doing so. You couldn't allow her to divorce you. You dared not risk any publicity. You started your foul, cruel campaign against her in the village hoping she'd just leave you. Why didn't you tell her she wasn't legally married to you?"

"And risk her running me in for bigamy? She was stupid but not as stupid as all that."

"She wanted to leave you. She wanted to marry Julian. She was carrying his child."

Wainwright was quite unmoved. Dr Frost saw, with loathing, that he was incapable of pity, of love, of feeling of any kind except for himself.

"So you arranged for Mrs Cowley to make you a poison you could put in some of Celia's capsules and you left it to chance when she would die."

Wainwright smiled faintly.

"She couldn't have picked a better time or place, could she? If those bums had left her alone it'd been suicide on account of the pregnancy and Farnham not wanting her. I meant it to look like that. They'll never really prove it was me, not Farnham, who switched the capsules."

"You realise you are making me a confession, don't you?"

"Who'll believe you? Interfering old beggar! You've got no proof. Cowley won't spill."

"Mrs Cowley is dead. She died this morning, when she heard that Mrs Winter had been found strangled."

Wainwright shrank a little.

"So that's why you're here?"

"Partly. But chiefly because I know why you strangled her. I know what she had to blackmail you with. Mrs Thompson has told me what she found. Celia's diary. Did she read one of your wife's letters? She'd realised the bigamy, hadn't she? She was going to expose you. She was going away with Julian in order to do that. She was frightened of you. She thought

185

you might kill her. So she hid the diary in her chimney. It wasn't a very sensible thing to do. Frightened people are not always sensible. She should have kept it with her. But she was terrified. She must have forgotten to take it, or perhaps she would have done that when she took her car home before she went away with Julian."

"She was stupid," Wainwright muttered. "I've always said it—stupid!"

"And innocent," Dr Frost said. "A born victim, my daughter Judy was told."

He looked at Wainwright. The old man was breathing hard, his lips were growing blue. Dr Frost went to him and felt his pulse.

"You'll have to be careful," he said. "Age tells in the end."

"Why don't you get the hell out?" Wainwright whispered.

Dr Frost went to the door and opened it. Mrs Wainwright was standing outside, her face white and drawn.

"You kept him on too tight a rein," he said sadly.

She rallied. She was not to be criticised, she said.

"If I hadn't held the purse strings we'd both have been ruined long ago," she insisted.

"That wasn't quite what I meant," he answered. But as he drove back to his hotel he realised that, to them, it was the good, sufficient reason for everything that had happened and was likely to happen, to them both.

Dr Frost travelled back to Upfold the next day. Superintendent Mitchell and his sergeant went down overnight by car. The information on the superintendent's desk related to a previous bigamy committed by Wainwright in Liverpool under the name of Stephens. The deserted 'wife' had recognised him in a newspaper photograph taken outside the coroner's court and after some hesitation had written to Scotland Yard, enclosing her long-cherished, false marriage lines. A few more details of this affair and the rapid assistance of Interpol, which had confirmed Wainwright's original and only legal marriage, had given Mitchell enough cause to send him off through the night to Cornwall.

But Wainwright was not in his home. Mrs Wainwright, roused from her bed at six in the morning by the police officers, had gone to her husband's room to find the bed unused and a short note on the pillow. Beside it an envelope, addressed to Mitchell, contained a very condensed confession of guilt.

Mrs Wainwright, speechless with shock and grief, held out her note.

"I'm best out of it for good," he had written. "You wouldn't have seen any more of me, anyway."

Just that. No expression of regret, of love, of gratitude. A mean reward for her devotion, her tenacity, her business acumen, her capital.

Mitchell handed it back and set about organising a search with the aid of the local police. They found sufficient relics, a little dump of jacket, wallet, and stick at the top of a high cliff, a sheer drop to the sea. Half way down a handkerchief had caught on a bush growing horizontally from a tiny ledge. It was quite enough. They could only wait for the body to be washed ashore, when an inquest would be held.

The superintendent returned to London, taking with him the written statement that would clear all other living suspects.

He was a very angry man. Again Dr Frost had interfered at a vital moment to baulk him. Really the old fool ought to be run in for obstruction. If he hadn't given the show away to Wainwright the murderer would by now be in custody and he himself once more successful in running down a criminal. As it was, the case was brought to an untidy end. Cutfield and Pawley would have to be charged with concealing a death and would get an appropriate punishment, but you couldn't prosecute a whole village. Farnham was a bit of a problem. He could be charged for the same offence as the farmer and his friend. But he had, however, late in the day, provided the real evidence of Celia's murder. Anyway, it wasn't his, Mitchell's, province to prosecute. It was a messy finish, most unsatisfactory.

"I suppose really it was you that drove him to suicide," said Mrs Frost, thoughtfully, a few weeks later.

"I don't think so," her husband answered.

"Why not? He saw the game was up after you'd seen him. He took the quickest way out."

"Oh yes, I think he did that."

"I don't know what you mean."

"I mean I don't think a handkerchief would catch on a bush from the inside of a trouser pocket falling past it. Nor fall out of a trouser pocket on its own. A jacket pocket, perhaps. But the jacket was on the top of the cliff."

"How did it get there, then? The handkerchief, I mean, in the bush?"

"Wrapped loosely round a stone? I don't know," said Dr Frost.

"I think you're trying to be too clever," Mrs Frost said. "Bodies in the sea often turn up *months* later. That man at Portsmouth and that playwright who fell off a ship."

"I think I'll plant out the wallflower seedlings," said Dr Frost, "after that nice shower we had in the night."

"Don't forget Judy and Julian will be down for lunch," his wife reminded him.

EPILOGUE

When Mr Wainwright had planted his jacket, wallet and keys at a likely spot on the cliff top a mile or so from his house and had watched the handkerchief, freed from the lump of turf he had wrapped it round, flutter out of sight in the darkness, he put on his raincoat and walked away through the night.

He walked fifteen miles, carrying a suitcase, to a small railway station, now disused, but from where he was able to take a workmen's bus into Truro. No mean achievement for a man of nearly seventy-eight.

He was wearing a cloth cap and his raincoat was old and shabby. Everyone on the bus, including the driver and conductor, was in an early morning mood, inclined to be sleepy, taciturn and unnoticing. Mr Wainwright made no impression on them whatever.

From Truro he took a train to Plymouth, where he retrieved at the left luggage department a larger suitcase he had deposited there in case of need on his way up to London ten days before. It contained clothes of all necessary kinds. The suitcase he carried held the five hundred pounds in notes he had given, in exchange for Celia's diary, to Mrs Winter before he strangled her and which he had taken back afterwards.

With these two pieces of luggage he went on board a passenger steamer bound for Brest, where he arrived the same evening. There he transferred to a French liner bound for Canada. He still had a few disreputable friends in the Dominion, upon whom he was relying to help him. It would be difficult for them to refuse to help him, he knew.

When the liner sailed, which it did a day later, Mr Wainwright, travelling now in the name of Brook, considered that as usual his flair, his phenomenal foresight, his incredible energy, had paid off as handsomely as usual. But he had forgotten one vital factor, his own age. His vanity, his self-absorption and self-confidence, had not allowed for it.

Halfway across the Atlantic his heart gave way, strained by the excitement and anxieties of the last two weeks, overworked by his physical exploits in driving a hired car to Upfold and back through one night, killing an active, middle-aged woman fighting for her life, and finally, after only two days' rest, walking fifteen miles carrying five hundred pounds in notes. He woke on the third morning out, fighting for breath. The ship's doctor, Gallic, laconic, warned him of acute danger. Later that day he knew that he had reached the end.

Gasping, he refused the ship's offer to have him flown back to England or on to Canada.

"I can do nothing here," the doctor said.

"I have no one to go to," Wainwright gasped. "I shall not live long enough. I'd rather die at sea than in a plane."

"As you wish," said the doctor.

During the afternoon, in response to treatment, Wainwright rallied, but he knew the relief was temporary. He asked to see the captain and tried to make him promise to bury him at sea. This the captain was unwilling to do until Wainwright assured him that there would be no one to receive his body on arrival. The doctor, foreseeing endless complications unless the dying man's wish was fulfilled, persuaded the captain to promise. It could be very private, the passengers need not know, only one or two of the crew. Wainwright, grinning at their agitated improvisations, was content. With his last remaining strength he passed the balance of his five hundred pounds of undeclared English currency through a porthole into the sea. He made a little will, leaving all his effects to his French friends in Brest.

He died peacefully at ten o'clock that night and was slipped overboard unobtrusively at midnight, the captain reading aloud, to the best of his ability, the Anglican service from a Prayer Book he had borrowed from a British traveller.

Mr 'Brook's' effects were sent to the address he had given. He had stayed at this small hotel several times over the years. They knew nothing about him beyond this fact. They were sorry. He had been charming. It was a charming, though strange, gesture to leave them his property. They disposed of the clothes, pocketed the money and burned the passport as a precaution.

So the true end of John Wainwright was never established with certainty. Superintendent Mitchell was no more deceived by the jacket and handkerchief than Dr Frost had been. But he was not quick enough. Besides, though the ports and airfields and Interpol were warned about a John Wainwright and a Geoffrey Stephens, Mitchell had not heard of a Hugh Brook. The bigamously married, untimely deserted, Mrs Brook in Halifax had not seen the photograph in the newspaper.

For regular early information

about

FORTHCOMING NOVELS

send a postcard

giving your name and address

in block capitals

to

THE FICTION EDITOR

HODDER & STOUGHTON LTD.,
St. Paul's House, Warwick Lane,
London, E.C.4.